"*Pipers and a Dancer* is so brilliant, and handled in so masterly a fashion, that one is carried away by the skill and wit and vivid imagery in the book . . . . One reads on and on in sheer delight."

The Bookman

"It is, we suppose, the most brilliant novel published this year; it contains more wit, more unruly intelligence than any English novel since the nineties."

The Spectator

"Miss Benson not only has genius, she knows how to control it. When she pipes no one sensitive to beauty can help dancing to her tune."

The Daily Graphic

Pipers and a Dancer

~ by the same author ~

I Pose (1915)
This is the End (1917)
Living Alone (1919)
The Poor Man (1922)
Pipers and a Dancer (1924)
The Little World (1925)
Goodbye, Stranger (1926)
Worlds Within Worlds (1928)
Tobit Transplanted (1931)
Pull Devil, Pull Baker (1933)
Mundos (1935)
Poems (1935)
Collected Short Stories (1936)

PIPERS AND A DANCER

by

STELLA BENSON

SANDNESS
MICHAEL WALMER
2023

Pipers and a Dancer first published 1924
This edition published 2023

by

Michael Walmer
North House
Melby
Sandness
Shetland ZE2 9PL

ISBN 978-0-6452440-6-9 paperback

CHAPTER I

IPSIE suddenly stopped speaking and heard with horror the echo of her own voice saying, " You see, I lost my three brothers in the War." " How damn pathetic," she thought, and she reminded herself for the thousandth time that she had determined to be reserved. No man ever told her half as much about himself as she told nearly all men about herself. This was why men were so seldom in love with her. Indeed, she thought, no one who knew her very well ever loved her much. Rodd, with whom she was sitting now on the starlit boat-deck, was not attracted by her. For the first two or three days out of San Francisco he had energetically sought her company, but now he did not seem much interested to learn that she was bereaved and lonely.

" Three brothers! " echoed Rodd in his agreeable edged American voice. " Why, that's terrible."

Ipsie decided finally that bereavement was not a charm and tried to say no more, but in a moment she added in a low voice, " Yes, it made a great difference to me."

Rodd asked for no further information and Ipsie offered none.

Ipsie was cruelly and deliciously obsessed by her Showman. All her life she had been exhibited by a showman before a ghostly and ideal public. She hated the Showman because his voice was almost always heard by fools. All his best perorations were only enjoyed by fools. And yet what he had to show was often good. The story of her lost brothers, for instance, was good.

Her eldest brother was killed in 1915— this was what she would have told Rodd if he had only had that rare but irresistible look in his eyes that tells of an hour to spare.

PIPERS AND A DANCER

In 1915 Ipsie was being exhibited by her Showman as a Rèd Cross worker. She kept a rather inaccurate card index and knew the name of every hospital in France. She wore a becoming white handkerchief round her head and a strained expression to match her disguise—the expression of one who never for a moment forgot her dear ones at the front and never for a moment forgot that she never forgot them. She wrote to a brother every day. Her letters were brave and boring, but her brothers were very kind about them. Even her second brother Conrad, who knew her, was kind about them. He always made allowances for the Showman.

Into Ipsie's office where a dummy death posed all day long, death was tossed carelessly. Her mother's voice on the telephone was very loud and false. " Ipsie, come home at once. Ipsie, come to me at once. Victor is dead."

Ipsie's Showman was master of the situation. She hoped that her face was pale as

she turned to the other girls. Pictorially
people in anguish have squared mouths, so
Ipsie's jaw stiffened. " My eldest brother
. . . dead." She did not, of course, think
that he was dead, though the Showman
clamoured about death. Actually a person
called Victor Wilson, who could move his
ears and could never brush his back hair
flat, could not possibly be dead. Victor
was dreadfully successful; surely death was
a weakness he could never have achieved.
Still, the idea was dramatic. It would be
tragic but dramatic if his electric model
gunboat were never to be finished.
Dramatic if Victor's head—the shell of that
accurate brain that knew all about electric
models and despised all artists but Kipling—
were even now bowed humbly to the mud.
The rain and the mud would flatten his
hair at last.

Ipsie's Showman stood by her. And for
that reason Victor was never dead to her.
She had loved him too little and respected
him too much. Simply—he never came

home. Death was held captive in his empty room with the half-finished model gunboat. Ipsie's Showman could chain up death.

Ipsie hated herself now—or rather her Showman of to-day hated the Showman of yesterday—when she remembered the letters she wrote to her two brothers after Victor's death. There was a " new depth " in them. " Ordeal by fire " . . . " we shall emerge new men " . . . etc., etc. Her brothers were still very kind about her letters. Only Philip, who, as his mother rightly said, was a little unfortunate in his disposition, wrote that he never had been a new man even when he was born; he was always second-hand and not a bargain at that—and after the War would not raise twopence halfpenny at a rummage sale. Philip was always depressed, always a tiresome person to talk nobly to. He was ugly and very slightly deformed; his family had never heard him express enthusiasm. His brothers and his sister were a little shy of him because he

5

was morbid and often sour. His mother was not in the least shy of him; on the contrary, she suggested often that he should take up stamps or some other hobby. She hoped that he might thus justify his bad manners. He was imaginative and not very clever. He was much occupied by thoughts of pain. His temper was so short that there never was an inch of it to spare. After he was wounded and before he died he wrote in the diary that had been his only friend, " Life to me has been physically a long battle, mentally a long intoxication, spiritually a long dream."

Ipsie's mother, her feather boa shivering on her thin shoulders, was in the hall starting for France to see the wounded Philip when the news came of his death. Ipsie's Showman had deserted her at that moment for the first time, and the picture printed for ever on her eyes included for the first time no Ipsie. It showed only her mother crouching and trembling a little as if she were cold, taking off her glasses helplessly after reading the telegram. There was a picture, too, of Philip with a happy face at last—the exultant face of a skull. There was a picture of Conrad left alone to face greedy death.

"Yes," said Ipsie to Rodd, leaning forward to keep her eyes on a star which the ship was leaving behind. "I was eighteen then. That was when I first met Jacob. He was terribly good to me. But we didn't get engaged at that time. . . ." The star interrupted her. She saw a star suddenly for the first time in her life. This experience often interrupted her. She often saw many things for the first time—some things almost for the time before the first time. Then she remembered Jacob Heming, fat and handsome, sitting in her mother's drawing-room with his finger-tips together, singing very wheezily, and at the end of each song suggesting another. "And then there's 'Loch Lomond' . . . how it carries me back . . . my old Grannie used to sing 'Loch Lomond.' . . . By yahn bahnie brakes. . . ."

7

He sang apparently for his own benefit but really for theirs in an almost voiceless but very sentimental whisper, swinging his head, tapping his finger-tips together, half shutting his eyes. Ipsie and her mother were of course too polite to talk of something else while the songs were going on. After he had gone Ipsie's mother once or twice said, " Well, Ipsie, all I can say is . . ." But she never said anything more, so perhaps that really was all she could say. Men were scarce and not very often attracted by Ipsie. Jacob was an electrical engineer and claimed to be a successful one. He had been a friend of Victor's, perhaps on electrical grounds.

" No," added Ipsie to Rodd. " He wrote years after and asked me to come out to China and marry him."

She wished that Rodd would say to her, " Do you really love him? " If he were somebody in a Russian novel he would. If he had asked her that, she would have said " No," but she would not have been able

8

to explain herself. For behind her eyes rather than within her brain seemed to lie all that was relevant to the unlikely question, " Ipsie, do you love . . . ? "

Men meant nothing to her, nothing more than Jacob Heming or Lord Salisbury or Anthony Trollope or the fishmonger, but Man she could see now with secret eyes, tall, pale-haired, thin and a little hesitating in the sentimental setting of a garden. Heliotrope dies so quickly when gathered and lives not long when rooted in common earth, but here in a sentimental garden it lives for ever, incense at the feet of perfection. " How dretfully, dretfully sentimental . . ." said Man, spearing his chin delicately with a spear of lavender. Ipsie could see him pull out his mouth into a parodied grin of sentiment. Part of his perfection was that he was a parody—in other words, a brother. There never had been a perfect man in the world except her brother Conrad. There was no perfect man in the world now.

9

PIPERS AND A DANCER

Rodd said, " Well, I'm naturally crazy to know Mr. Heming after all you've told me. And he'll surely be crazy to know me and get all the latest news about you."

" I don't suppose you'll be long together," said Ipsie. She imagined Jacob and Rodd sitting opposite to each other and Jacob saying, " Then there's ' When Irish Eyes are Smiling '—do you ever hear these quaint old songs in the States? " Rodd would think, " What on earth was that cute little fairy of a girl thinking of? . . . why it's a perfect crime. . . ."

Jacob was not coming to Hongkong to meet Ipsie. He had to stay in Yunnan long enough to hand over to Rodd, his successor.

" I don't suppose we will be long together," said Rodd, sleepily pleasant. " I guess he's got his trunks packed ready the moment this ship was scheduled to leave San Francisco. I'll be nothing more than the word Go to him."

He always said what he thought would

please unless he consciously checked himself. He very much liked being liked.

The talk, Ipsie admitted reluctantly, was at an end. " He says such unintimate things, yet I know he could if he liked. . . ." She must send him away before he could suggest going. " There are the poker people looking for you. I'm going for a walk round the deck before I go down and pack."

. He did not say, " I'd rather walk with you than play poker."

Ipsie, alone, stood watching the sea. She thought of her drawing—*New People in Monterey*—lately reproduced in *Paint*. She imagined people all over the world turning over the pages of *Paint* and catching their breath as they reached her page. Especially she imagined the face of Conrad, lost in the delight of her work. She did not consciously think a very great deal about Conrad now that he was dead. She sustained no arguments against herself; her . thoughts were so incurious that she had never wondered what had become of him; she had never shared her mother's wish to " get in touch " with him; she had never confronted herself with the fact that actually he obsessed her. Only he was Man in the innocent teeming world of her eyes. He was her instinctive protest against a world in which perfection has no being. Ipsie's eyes perhaps were mad. They dominated her thoughts and yet their emphasis was false. Her eyes had dreams but they had no vision. Her hysterical ingenuity in reproducing line was her only form of expression. Her reason was devoured by the things her eyes had seen and were seeing and might see if prophecies could come true and remembered lovelinesses return. For her the sea to-night was not water but a great snare of lines that held her fast. For her the fields of the sky by night or by day were always unexplored and in them she must always lose her way. Hers was an easy way to lose. She saw and expressed more than she

knew. This made her rather a popular
artist with the readers of *Paint* and their
kind. Her innocence of intellectual intention induced a kind of spacious suspense
in her work which was most useful to young
connoisseurs who had a great deal of intellectual intention to spare.

CHAPTER II

IPSIE looked in the mirror in her cabin as the ship swung into dock opposite Hong-kong. She thought that her face was the work of a beginner. Of course, this ought not to matter very much to-day since Jacob Heming would not be there to appraise her. Still, the Showman would have liked Rodd to carry away a beautiful undying memory. Nothing was less likely, she thought. Some people's faces were somehow inevitable, whether they were beautiful or ugly. They were bravely made; their lines could be seen from any angle without surprise. Ipsie's eyes were small, rather sunken, and would not open widely. There seemed to be no bones in her face. Sometimes when she stood on deck near the engine she was ashamed to feel her cheeks, her chin and the tip of her nose trembling like jelly with the vibration.

Ipsie went on deck to meet a wonderful young man who should come up to her and say, " I know you, Ipsie Wilson; you drew that wonderful thing in *Paint—New People in Monterey*. I know you, and I know the New People, because I too have sheltered under the eaves of those waves."

The wonderful young man could not be expected yet as the ship's gangways were not down. Only Rodd was waiting about, wearing a remote-looking hat never seen before. Rodd never seemed to know that Ipsie was an artist though she had told him so several times in the deprecatory voice her Showman had taught her.

The ship was flirting with the dock; she turned away yet sidled nearer. The edge of the dock was trimmed with a sort of dull lace of other people's friends. Opposite, across the water, the stout pillars of Hong-kong's mountains were holding up a taut sky. So early was the morning that all colour lay under a film of white sunlight. A jellyfish, intense jade green under the glassy water, threw all Ipsie's world out of perspective for a little while.

Ipsie crossed the deck again, escaping from the dangerous jellyfish. As she did so she imagined herself as she would appear to the wonderful young man; she would be leaning over the rail, her round face white with excitement under her new black boyish hat. She would not see him, she decided, until he had looked at her for some minutes. When Ipsie caught herself imagining such adventures she usually checked herself. " Just like a flapper in the Strand," she thought. But to-day she was come to China to be married. The super-flapper was come to the greater Strand.

" Don't you think anyone 'll come to meet you, Miss Wilson? " asked Rodd Innes.

" Yes — didn't I tell you ? — Pauline Heming, Jacob's sister. She lives in Hong-kong. She has a business position here."

PIPERS AND A DANCER

Pauline had never mattered at all; she had scarcely appeared in Ipsie's secret prophecies. Women were very seldom adventures. They were either too easily impressed by Ipsie's Showman or else they refused to join in the tableau at all. The most one could say was that women were nothing at all in advance. Yet now, when it seemed that there was no possible man or woman for Ipsie in the row of smiling friends on the edge of the wharf, Ipsie was so much disappointed that her thoughts rushed home to her mother—a rather absurd figure to be so stupendously removed from her by violent seas. She imagined her mother looking gentle, slim, whaleboned, pursed; the rather over-fluffy feather boa would be held down by a plain mushroom hat advertised as " matron's travelling wear." She would look what she was, an underfed, impecunious widow. Imagining her mother's old black alpaca dress, her mother's withered and conservative face, her mother's thin grey hair (augmented after much sincere doubt by a switch of a rather too steely shade of grey), contracted Ipsie's cold heart. Mothers, she thought, are seen to unfair advantage across thousands of miles of sea.

"My God!" said Rodd as two young women with peroxide bobbed hair and an unbobbed expanse of silk leg rushed on board and kissed some hitherto respectable fellow-passengers. "I hope nobody will kiss me."

Ipsie was on the contrary sorry to find that nobody intended to kiss her. She went back to look for the jelly-fish but it was gone. She had to re-create it for herself.

A splashing sampan ploughed through the radiance shed by the remembered jelly-fish. In the sampan sat three passengers, but chiefly a very tall vivid woman in dark red, leaning at rather an awkward angle towards Ipsie.

"Ipsie Wilson—little sister Ipsie. . . . That must surely be you. Wait—I'll be with you."

PIPERS AND A DANCER

The sampan vanished abruptly under the fat black hams of the ship.

" There, you see," said Ipsie to herself. " I'm just like other people after all."

Pauline's voice came rolling like a banner in front of her heavily hurrying figure. " I missed the ferry. Oh, how could I run such a risk of leaving my little new sister lonely in a strange land! Ipsie, Ipsie, half Hongkong's dying to meet you, and here's a deputation to tell you so. Here's Pennell Norman—Captain Norman, to introduce him properly. Here's Mrs. Sophie Tooloose Hinds, an American writer —who loves Jacob very nearly as much as you do."

" Miss Wilson, very happy to meet you."

Very happy . . . very happy. . . . Ipsie's hands were somehow full of roses. " Dear little sister from far away," said Pauline in her deep rather unwieldy voice, and pressed Ipsie's shoulder against one of her breasts. Ipsie felt intensely embarrassed and intensely pleased. She was not an expert in affection; she was usually at a loss for the bare words of love, but she would have tried gratefully to clasp some part of the large Pauline had not her hands been full of roses.

Mrs. Hinds beamed at Ipsie through pince-nez and bubbled her joy through thin lips, but Ipsie made no reply. Americans see English people always reduced to dumbness on a first introduction; they must think us an oddly inarticulate race. However, I suppose they remember William Shakespeare and Ethel M. Dell and hope for the best.

As they all walked towards the ferry, Ipsie, in a ring of kind faces all at a rather higher level than her own, felt herself physically and spiritually to be a " sweet little thing." Pauline imposed this feeling on her and Ipsie was not cynical enough to throw it off easily. Ipsie's face assumed a pert childish look and she began to think of sweet little things she might say about Hongkong in order to make them all laugh affectionately again. Ipsie could feel this sweetness coming on remorselessly like an attack of indigestion or a swelling after a mosquito bite. "Hang it all," she said to herself irritably. "I'm not sweet and I won't be little. Where am I all this time? What is this person in my skin?" Being charming, she thought, is generally somehow cheating. She therefore said nothing at all as the ferry carried her and her friends over the satin water to the feet of the island of Hongkong.

Pauline looked imperiously established in a world in which Ipsies and the majority of persons under five foot eleven moved doubtfully. Pauline's hair, her cheeks and her mouth were full of colour and life; it was inconceivable that she should ever have suffered from adenoids or bad teeth or colds in the nose or pimples or any of those afflictions which print a disappointing oddity on the faces of less fortunate persons.

Ipsie found herself in a carrying-chair for which, unfortunately, she was too light.

PIPERS AND A DANCER

The two chair-bearers seemed to be maliciously bouncing along, and Ipsie was thrown up and down until her stomach ached. She enjoyed herself, however, and thought that she would draw an impression—*First Arrival in Hongkong*—in sunshiny zigzags. Pauline strode vigorously beside the chair. "I've seen some of your drawings reproduced in *Paint*. My little genius of a sister. You'll find I've done wonders as a publicity agent in Hongkong."

"Oh, I'm nothing but a puddler," gasped Ipsie bouncily from the chair. But she saw with regret a shadow of reproof on Pauline's face. Her rather posed humility had dimmed Pauline's enthusiasm. "I haven't got any temperament," added Ipsie.

"Sophie Hinds is an artist too—an artist to her finger-tips."

"That means an amateur," thought Ipsie scornfully. "My finger-tips have been found wanting."

Pauline's flat, about a fifth of the way up the Peak, looked down on a beautiful maze of roofs and ships and striped water. Across the water were hills. The spines of the hills were abruptly faded as though the seams of their clothes had worn threadbare. Pauline's rooms were purposefully gaudy; her dark and eager presence glowed against a rather trivial glare of canary colour and sealing-wax red. Mirrors in vermilion frames taunted the human face with its lack of the primary colours. Ipsie threw herself on to a rather too ephemeral pile of purple and orange cushions on a divan. She said, " But what a beautiful man Captain Norman is ! "

Now suddenly the whole pleasure of this comment was spoilt by Captain Norman's own voice saying, " Oh, please, please . . ." He had been standing by the doorway looking at a picture of a Madonna and thinking it was rather like Pauline. Pauline meant people to think this. That was why she had hung it there.

Ipsie's clothes seem to stick to her for a moment with heat and embarrassment.

But Pauline laughed a loud noble contralto laugh and said, " The artist's unfailing eye, Pennell. Don't take the compliment as personal."

" Better 'n if you'd said the other thing," mumbled Captain Norman, looking amiably at Ipsie. He was very much pleased, of course, and was too stupid to be much embarrassed.

" Anyway, let's talk about something else," said Ipsie.

Mrs. Hinds, panting from her climb, was in the room now. She had a small wrinkled colourless face in a fade-out effect of white hair. Her nose was nearly flat, but pince-nez clung mystically to a bridge that was hardly there. She obviously adored Pauline. When Pauline spoke, the expression on Mrs. Hinds' face reflected that on Pauline's with a touch of distortion, like a parody. Ipsie thought that Mrs. Hinds seemed adjusted and held for inspection; her high-heeled feet seemed to stand on tenterhooks. When she should be alone surely she would let

24

her brisk face go and her pince-nez would fall off and her wiry white hair would droop limply.

She and Pauline flirted with epigrams.

" Masterman Earle's here. . . . You've heard of Masterman Earle, of course. : . ."

" No, I'm afraid . . ."

" A painter by trade, an avenging angel by calling, a consumptive by mistake."

" And what shall we say of Christina? " asked Mrs. Hinds, obviously giving Pauline a cue.

" Christina's a beautiful ugly Boston bulldog of a woman. If she loved him less she'd marry him; if she loved him more she'd leave him."

Nearly all the pearls of wisdom were un-mistakably Parisian.

" Oh, wine, women, and song. . . . Why are we always numbered among the vices and only second place at that? "

What interesting people they tried to be! Ipsie could find no comments. Impersonal eloquence seemed to her miraculous.

PIPERS AND A DANCER

Captain Norman watched the three women from under frowning hairy brows. "Not shy," thought Ipsie, "but full of hatred." She was wrong. But she had to imagine him rather maliciously for herself. Inspired by an unconscious instinct of revenge she posed Norman in trivial humble attitudes. She thought of him in a crowded shop choosing that dull but gentlemanly tie. She thought of him eating in a restaurant so crowded that the man sitting back to back with him could feel him swallow. She thought of him trying to pull over his head a shirt which wouldn't go on because the washerwoman had buttoned it up. She thought of him running for a bus and missing it. Her imagination dethroned him from the high judgement seat of silence in which he was ensconced.

"My little new sister is pale with excitement and fatigue," boomed Pauline. "You must both go away and leave us to rest and get acquainted."

As they assembled about the door Ipsie

26

heard Captain Norman's voice — " Yes, rather. She's fascinating." Usually to hear that one is fascinating is to know oneself sadly on the wrong side of the footlights. Ipsie felt this, but she was glad that it had been said. " Now I shall know him after all. I needn't feel strained. He will come back without my contriving."

CHAPTER III

Rodd Innes in the train rattling northward through Tonkin to Yunnan sat up stiffly. His face was rather dirty and his hair full of coal-dust. He had an obstinate short face and smiling shallow eyes. He was an obstinate and tender-hearted creature, never bored and never ecstatically interested. He had a slight gentle contempt for most people because they were so easily attracted and amused by him. He had no fear of being conventional and was therefore able to be compassionate and to behave with an imaginative kindness rare in much more imaginative men.

He played solitaire with a cheerful persistence. For four years he had been trying in spare moments of travel to find a pack of cards in such a mood that, after certain shiftings, they would allow themselves to be piled in sequence in four heaps. Cards were obstinate, but not more obstinate than was Rodd. He intended to wring surrender from the cards before he died. He never cheated at solitaire. He neither analysed nor cheated himself in any circumstances. He had a few isolated shreds of imagination. He personified cards, his clothes, and occasional details connected with his work. In typing *Iodide*, for instance, he would pause at *Io* and think to his typewriter—" There, you thought I had made a mistake—10 with a small naught—you're wrong — now watch. . . ." But when he had added *dide* he did not realise that he had enjoyed this scarcely perceptible triumph. He did not know that he knew that the King of Spades was an ardent admirer of the late President Roosevelt and that the Queen of Diamonds was a frigid shrew.

His determination to do the right thing

now made him put his cards away and look
out of the window as a traveller should.
He thought that he was lost for ever. He
would be attached to the world now by
nothing more binding than that continuous
chain of heavily flowering creepers that ran,
it seemed, all the way from the coast of
Tonkin to the mountains of southernmost
China. He would surely never be able to
extricate himself from such a tangle of
templed swamps and small sharp-plumed
hills and strangled trees.

The train ran like a struggling fish on
an almost taut line; it jerked helplessly
yet strongly from side to side; twitching
and tugging, it was drawn through the
rippling land towards the ruthless mountains.
The moment, the hour, the day, were all
extremely uncomfortable and held nothing
to look forward to. But Rodd was American
and was therefore sustained by the conscientious statistical form of interest common
to the tourists of his race. " I'm seeing a
land that less than one-hundredth of one

per cent of the citizens of Boston have ever seen. I needn't be too darn truthful in my letters home." Also he thought that some very interesting or astonishing thing might happen to him at any moment. To be so far lost was to be found by strangeness.

Rodd was one of the few persons who really profited by the discovery of Drake or Magellan or Columbus or whoever it was that established the globularity of the globe. Rodd actually was inarticulately conscious of himself as a little essential louse moving about an immense but quite conceivable round object. In most people's minds their flat world opens like a school atlas which is shut nearly all the time. When it is open they can find the names of the places they have been to or have cousins in, underlined in red like minor British colonies. But Rodd was almost aware of the whole real world, a world spotted with towns and trees and mountains rather than with names, a world faintly but perceptibly smudged with the louse-like footprints of himself

crawling and crawling about it. His geo-
graphical mind was limited to this planet,
so that his globe, not being seen relatively,
was always stationary. The continent of
America, when looked at, as always, from
the North Pole, was on his left, slipping
down a little towards Europe; the Pacific
was the spine of the fat carcase of the world,
and Asia covered the right ribs. Under
the belly were Russia, the Balkan States
and other usually invisible regions. Tourists'
Europe, comprising France, Germany, Italy,
Scandinavia and England, patched the left
lower ribs.

The train across Tonkin was now running
down from the spine and one could see the
ribs ahead, the mountains of China, harsh
in the late light. The low sun had freed
itself from a devouring storm of clouds only
to find itself in danger of being drowned in
rough mountains.

At Laokay, the edge of Indo-China, the
train stops for the night looking across the
river to China and the mountains that it

must attack next day. The mountains after the sunset were like dark flames, so steep and pointed were they. A small noiseless rain was falling. The hot air seemed to hold down and suffocate sound. After twelve hours in the train Rodd felt as if the world were empty. His footsteps, gritting on the road, rang to the sky.

Everything was very uncomfortable. People who were not American seemed deliberately to avoid efficiency or comfort, Rodd thought. No American—not even a first generation American—would have tolerated as a part of his existence in a strange land hotels like this—trains like this—regulations like this—pigs like this on railway stations—beards like this on officials—Americans were people who wanted to leave every place better than they found it, to leave every man more of a man than they found him. (They might even have brought back manliness to the Tonkinese.) Americans could open doors to almost all that was admirable—it was their misfortune, not their fault, that movies and victrolas and advertisements squeezed in when they opened the door.

Rodd sat on the damp verandah of the hotel and watched the *légionnaires* arguing, sitting bent towards one another in acute irascible angles, their foreheads and the sockets of their eyes wet with heat and irritation. The men of the Foreign Legion bring their own worlds with them from their own places; their only common ground is intoxication.

An Englishman who had been sitting with his wife at a neighbouring table came up to Rodd and said, " English, eh? "

" American," said Rodd, pleasantly. He rarely expressed criticism or reproach. He kept to himself his mild comment on the stranger's lack of observation, " At least I thought my clothes fitted me."

" English or American—it's all the same in Yunnan," said the Englishman. " Come and meet my wife and have a drink."

The stranger was very tall and thin and

his narrow bald head leaned backward rather than forward. His mouth, which was habitually open, seemed to emphasise the backward tilt of his head. The wife, to whose table Rodd allowed himself to be led, had a mincing, cautiously appealing face.

" Going to Yunnan-fu? "

" No.   Yueh Lai Chou."

" Well now . . . we come from there."

" I'm going up to take over the electrical plant there."

" Heming's job? "

" Yes, do you know him? "

" My goodness gracious! " exclaimed the stranger's wife. " You'll have to mess with Heming for a bit. He isn't leaving for ten days."

" Well? " asked Rodd. " You speak as if I weren't likely to survive it."

The Englishman gave a high foolish laugh. " You wait," he said. His wife giggled. They seemed to the American to be insanely inarticulate. " Nobody likes Heming at Yueh Lai Chou."

" But why not? "

" Oh, I don't know. . . . He's a priceless bore. You can't get rid of him—especially just before meal-times. . . . He's a
snob. . . . Stingy as a mule too. . . . He
tells long priceless stories—get him to tell
you the one about Maidie at Panama. . . .
He never has an idea how ridiculous he's
making himself. . . . If I lived with him
I'd poison his whisky on the third day."

Rodd characteristically bent to the breeze.
" Evidently I've a mean ten days ahead of
me," he said amiably. But secretly he
refused to dislike Heming—yet. He was
a very just young man.

His companions laughed a great deal.
The man had a laugh like whooping-cough
adapted for the purposes of merriment.
They were rather primitive people.

" What's the rest of the bunch up there
like? "

" Oh, they're all cads. Some worse than
others."

" But none much better, I understand."

PIPERS AND A DANCER

The stranger's wife laughed automatically whenever Rodd spoke. But now she wanted to say something, so she broke off the last moan of her laughter. " I must tell you a frightfully good story about Heming. You know, he's engaged to be married and——"

" Yes, I came over with her on the ship from San Francisco," said Rodd.

" Oh. . . ." The story was obviously spoilt.

" What is the good story? "

" Oh well . . . nothing—except that he showed us her photograph . . . he talked of her as a wee fairy, and she looks to have such a fat dull face in the photograph . . . and he's fat too."

" What is she like? " asked the husband presently, yawning.

Rodd was angry for Ipsie. She had seemed to him a precarious performer in the world's circus, tremulously balanced on a very thin wire. The audience obviously mattered to her too much. He felt remote from her in sympathy yet sorry for her, as a man might feel seeing a missionary girl palely approaching a big drunkard. The sneer of this flaccid giggling woman angered him.

" Do you want to know what she really seems like the way I see her, or do you want me to say—' Why, she's all right, but her face *is* rather round '? "

" Oo, he just wants to know what she looks like," said the woman. " You're not one of these dreadful people who can see into people's souls, are you? "

" She's a small person and looks mostly like a baby that hasn't quite enough to cry for and so decides to laugh. She has quiet-coloured hair that doesn't curl any. She wears the loveliest clothes—very prim and fine coloured, stiff and Colonial, someway. She talks a great deal in a sort of a hazy voice, as if she knew she was going to regret talking."

" How killing! But is she really like a fairy? "

" Perhaps a little bit," said Rodd gravely.

CHAPTER IV

MUCH excited by his splendid and strange journey, Rodd set foot on the platform of Yueh Lai Chou. The journey through the mountains since the train had entered China had been like a dream of a voyage across enchanted seas. The wild flowing mountains seemed always to be about to break upon his absurd craft; always, as mountain rose behind mountain, there was the sea-worshipper's wonder—*Shall I weather this next one . . . will this beautiful monster be my murderer . . .?* Leaning out of the carriage window one seemed to leave the train in its tunnel of noise and dust and to be moving aloof through a flowery silence that was edged by the sharp song of a bird. The enchanted sea was held spellbound by the bird's song; the great waves of land were lifted up and held, an ecstatic offering to the sky and the hesitating music. In all that great storm of still green earth, only the flowers moved, swinging in the scented wind.

Rodd bustled out of the train looking for objects whereby he could prove to himself deliciously that he really was in China. He sought things that he could mention casually in letters home, pretending they were commonplaces. The town of Yueh Lai Chou, which, from a distance, had looked like an island of dark trees in a great lake of flooded rice-fields, now declared itself as a round walled city, full, presumably, of houses that were too low to look over the wall. A couple of horned pagodas and three tall gatehouses—these alone stood up to see the world. A ring of pale bronze mountains leaned back placidly against the sky all round the broad valley in which the town stood.

There seemed to be no one at the station to meet Rodd, and the American, who, being

American, was used to being welcomed and befriended, was surprised but, being Rodd, not irritated.

A Chinese servant handed him a note addressed to Rodd Innes, Esquire, in a cramped clerklike handwriting.

Sorry I cannot meet you. Boy will show you the way. No need to hire a chair.—Heming.

Behind the boy, but in front of a file of coolies carrying his neat luggage, Rodd walked with his light rather conceited gait. His way, an unevenly paved road, led along the outer foot of the wall of Yueh Lai Chou. The late sun glared on the wall and on the small primitive faces of the soldiers leaning out to spit between the castellations at the top of the wall. Far away a bugle sounded, imperfectly played but attenuated and exciting. The bell at one corner of a pagoda rang desultorily in a light warm breeze.

The wall curved away from the road, faithful to the limit of the crouching city. And now Rodd walked beside a lake on which there were pink and white lotuses,

some closed like fists and some opening
like hands. Tonkinese women—for this
was their part of the city—were doing their
washing in the lake. Their black enamelled
teeth made their mouths look like gashes;
they all wore bright chestnut-coloured robes
and big straw trays balanced as sunshades
all awry on their neat black turbans. A
blind musician in a blue robe, led by a little
boy, met and passed Rodd, playing a thin
misty song, the only end or beginning of
which was the limit of hearing.

A gate beside which were written the
words *Electric Company of Yueh Lai Chou*
opened from the path that ran round the
lake. The gate looked across at a little hex-
agonal three-storied pagoda. The rippling
red, gold and green tiles of the pagoda
threw the bright fragments of sunlight about
as though they were water. Behind the
pagoda the brown mountains leaned against
the sky like old complacent paunchy men
paternally leaving the stage to young
creatures.

PIPERS AND A DANCER

Rodd, led by the boy, passed one of the windows of Heming's house before he reached the door. And a glance into the room showed him a big man—Heming, of course—sitting at a table sprawling forward, face downward, on the green cloth, hands out, in an attitude of despair.

The sight brought all Rodd's trivial excitement to a shocking standstill. There seemed to be no answer to such a greeting as that unconscious abandonment; nothing that he had heard of Heming seemed to fit this first glimpse. It was only after a second— long enough for the word *drunk* to have passed through Rodd's vaguely irritated mind—that the American moved forward to the door.

Jacob Heming, after a moment, came to the door. He was a heavy, high-shouldered man of forty, with a handsome though much too large face. His black thin hair stood up in little damp curls. His expression, in spite of his attitude of a moment ago, was not tragic—perhaps could not be tragic. It was sullen and a little vacant.

43

PIPERS AND A DANCER

" I'm glad to see you," he said, without eagerness. " I couldn't come to meet you because I was too busy. I'm having a big tea-party to-morrow as I'm going so soon. Lucky you've come in time for it."

The tinkling word tea-party coming from that big, unhappy man again roused Rodd's sense of irritation and strangeness.

The room in which he found himself was full of meaningless things. Cheap modern Chinese embroideries tried to conceal the fact that the furniture was only wicker. Even the gramophone had a skirt on; there was so much Nottingham lace on the windows that the colour was taken out of the sunset outside. On the walls were some coloured pictures of comic puppies and an Art Photograph of a lady very much like the " Soul's Awakening " but with nothing on.

All the time Rodd was unpacking his clothes in the dirty room allotted to him, he was groping for a thought that he had lost. Thoughts, mislaid like this, have

tastes as clues. A funny thought, a piece
of flattery, a definite wholesome decision, a
hope of a fair opportunity, even when lost,
all leave various sweet tastes on the mind.
But Rodd's lost thought was sour like
the thought of a quarrel or a dread or a
humiliation.

It was only when he had given up the
search for his thought and was looking for
a clean drawer in which to keep his hand-
kerchiefs, that he was suddenly able to name
the secret sour annoyance on his mental
palate.

" Ipsie Wilson—and this man. . . ."

" He may be quite a good fellow," he
answered himself. " And she needs some
horse-sense."

Rodd was a hopeful lazy creature, and
in spite of a tepid shave and the discovery
that he had left his ivory shoe-horn at
Laokay, he came cheerfully to dinner. All
round the dining-table were little tables,
and on each table was a pack of cards.

" For the tea-party," explained Heming,

45

who was already leaning over his soup. " I thought I'd better get it all ready to-day so as to be able to show you round the plant to-morrow. I've planned to have a Whist Drive. That ought to suit everybody. What do you think? "

" That'll be fine," said Rodd rather temperately. " People still play Whist in China, do they? In the States we don't much, except at Church Socials."

" I've never attended a Whist Drive in China—that's why I thought it would come rather fresh. In Glasgow all we young folks used to enjoy Whist Drives. I remember I once won a solid silver photo-frame."

" I'll bet you never found a picture that would fit it—one never does," said Rodd.

" I had one of myself that was exactly the right size."

Rodd wanted to shout *Ha-Ha* and bang his plate with his spoon to break the un-natural shell of chatty politeness that enclosed them. Tit-tat, Tit-tat—you say something

—I'll say something—it was as even and innocuous as the bleatings of a ewe and her lamb.

"About this tea-party," continued Heming. "You will be thinking as I'm not leaving till the end of next week it's rather soon to be giving a good-bye party."

Rodd thought, "I don't like thoughts put into my mouth." The emphasis laid on the tea-party seemed to him almost insane, but this may have been because he had spent the day with mountains.

"The reason I'm giving it so soon is to let them all know I'm really going. . . . You'll find a good many things in Yueh Lai Chou that'll set you thinking, Innes, and one of them is the extraordinary meanness of the people here—my God, stingy's not the word. . . ."

Rodd had some difficulty in coping with this statement. There seemed to be a hiatus in the sense. A Whist Drive—because the neighbours are stingy. . . . What —revenge?

PIPERS AND A DANCER

" So your entertainment's going to set good example? " he said brightly, taking leap in the dark and not much concerne with where he might land.

" In a manner of speaking—yes. It' not only for my own sake I have to try an assert myself. I have my position to kee up—the Company's position to keep up, a you might say. Now when the Riddell went away five people gave farewell feed for them. I've been here eighteen month and if you'll believe me—I've never bee inside the French Consul's dining-room... I dined with the bank manager once, an a rotten bad dinner it was too. . . . Th Marrowbys once asked me, and actually ha the cheek to put me in a worse place tha Fontanet—a damned number three in th railway. Now I'm going away, and I'n damn well going to let them all know it."

Rodd was silent, and for some tim Heming contented himself with munching fish irascibly, occasionally tearing a fish bone from his mouth with a fiendish grin

48

PIPERS AND A DANCER

" In Yueh Lai Chou you'll find you have to fight every inch of your way—nobody treats you right in a place like this unless you assert yourself."

Behind all Rodd's astonishment and mockery was the conviction—" He's miserable. Rightly or wrongly, he's horribly miserable." Whatever this solemn ridiculous man might say he still remained the man Rodd had first seen—disarmed—prostrate at the feet of misery.

" I mean it. You simply have to fight," said Heming. " Even the Chinks, seeing a foreigner slighted by other foreigners, are naturally only too ready to slight him too. Even one's own servants. The Chink magistrate here too—well, I'll have to tell you about him to-morrow, for that's all in the way of business. If I've caught these Chinks red-handed cheating the Company of light once, I've caught them a hundred times—but d'you think that magistrate'll sentence them?—not a bit of it. It's just fight, fight, fight, every yard of the way, and that you'll learn. As for the French neighbours—this party of mine's simply giving them an opportunity to do their duty by me. I'm just as good a man as Riddell any way, and he had *five* farewell feeds."

" Did I tell you I came over from San Francisco in the same ship as Miss Wilson?" asked Rodd after a pause, in a brisk doctor's bedside voice.

" Well now, to think of me forgetting that," said Heming more mildly. " Dear little Mary . . . how was she looking? I expect she's counting the days down there in Hongkong. She'll be cheery enough staying with my sister Pauline, though. Fine woman, Pauline; did you meet her? My, she had a fine education. An uncle of ours took a fancy to her and sent her all over the place—Brussels, Munich, Weston-super-mare. . . . Too much education for a woman really—not that I grudge her her advantages—Glasgow's good enough for me. But all that education unsettles a

woman — prevented Pauline marrying, I
always say. However, she's self-supporting
—got a good job as buyer for a big London
firm of importers. She and Mary'll get
along splendidly—all kinds of high-falutin
talk about art and so forth."

"I thought Miss Wilson signed her
name——"

"Oh yes, she's got a fancy name too—
Hippolyta. . . . Goes with her painting
and all that. Women soon give up these
fal-lals once they're married. Her first name
—Mary—is good enough for me. How
did you and wee Mary get on? She's a
cosy little body, isn't she? Old-fashioned
little soul too. You could count on her,
I always say."

"Her body is cosy, her soul old-fashioned."
It was like a dirge chanted in Rodd's head.
"It's her own affair," he told himself
dubiously.

He was awakened next morning by the
sound of clamorous voices in the next room.

PIPERS AND A DANCER

The voices scratched viciously across the
smooth morning air.   There was no argu-
ment, there was a duet of shouting for a
few minutes and then the sumph-sumph
of blows.

"The 'prentice fighter," Rodd called
himself as he stood up and, shivering a little
in his pyjamas, opened the door.

Heming and his Chinese boy, grinning
with anger, were leaning towards each other
almost in an attitude of passionate love.
The boy, who had evidently been hit, was
craning towards his master;   his hands
clawed towards him and his face looked as
though he might bite.

"Can I help?" asked Rodd mildly.

"Look at that for a servant," shouted
Heming, shaking his fist first at Rodd by
mistake and then at the boy.   "Look
what the bloody fool's done.   Put away all
the preparations for the tea-party.   All the
card-tables and the scoring papers. . . . I
put them all ready so as I'd have time to
take you round to-day. . . . What the

devil did the gaping swine think I took all that trouble for? . . . It's just as I told you —there's a conspiracy here to put slights and annoyances on me—every one's in it—the French Consul—the magistrate—my own servants. I can tell them I'm not the man to stand it. There's trouble coming."

"Let it come right now," interrupted Rodd. "Go right ahead. Make him put 'em all back. What time's breakfast?"

To see a Chinese in that state of desperate fury had quite shaken Rodd. He had not realised that any sounds but those of courtesy and laughter ever rose to Chinese lips. "I suppose Heming is one of these British Imperialists," he sighed as he returned to his room to dress.

All day the shadow of the tea-party lay upon the house, and by four o'clock Rodd had become so nervous that he put on one of his highest and least comfortable collars in order to be worthy.

"I got some little prizes together," said Heming. "I didn't buy them—I happened

53

to have them—prizes for deck games and such-like I've won from time to time and kept, knowing they'd come in handy for just such an occasion as this."

Rodd was thinking, " If I wrote Ipsie Wilson an exact account of everything said and done since I arrived here, and had it certified and stamped *vraisemblable* by the French Consul—would she still wait for him in Hongkong? "

" A metal matchbox, you see," said Heming. " Not silver, I believe—but if it was good enough for first prize for Bull-board on the *Fortuna*, it's good enough for first prize at a Whist Drive. Probably be won by a Frenchie anyway. Then this pencil-case—I never knew I had that till I found it in an old lacquer box I hadn't looked at for years. Just the very thing, I thought. I reckoned these little vases would do for the ladies. . . ."

They sat down at a card-table facing each other in a tense light of expectation.

" I haven't given a really grand entertain-

ment like this since I came to Yueh Lai
Chou," said Heming. " I've told the cook
to make two large plates of cakes—d'you
think that'll be enough? French people
very often don't touch cakes in the afternoon,
and then there's good food wasted."

" How many are we expecting? "

" Twenty-four if they all come."

" I feel quite rattled," said Rodd. " Tell
me about your plans. Talk to me or I
shall go insane with suspense, and begin
driving Whist alone."

" My plans," said Heming seriously.
" Well, my wedding in Hongkong is my
first plan. Then I have an offer of a fine
position in Shanghai which I think I shall
accept. Shanghai'd be a nice gay place
for Mary. And the manager of the plant's
a friend of Mary's brother, Victor Wilson.
Did Mary tell you about Victor? "

" She said that her brothers were all
killed in France."

" Yes, quite a tragedy. Victor was the
one I knew; he was a great loss. He was

a mechanical genius. Though they'd sent him to some fancy school—Harrow, I think—and he'd had no technical training, he had nearly as much grasp of practical science as I have with all my experience. A genius—no other word for it. Some of these Frenchies ought to be coming now. It's a quarter to five."

He walked to the window and looked out across the lake. There was a great cloud towering over Yueh Lai Chou. A thick pillar of rain at the far end of the valley erased a section of the distance and broke the circle of surrounding mountains. The city cowered under the tall cloud, Rodd thought, just as he himself cowered under the impending party.

" No one in sight, yet," said Heming. " What were we saying? Ah, the Wilsons. . . . It was, of course, through Victor Wilson that I ran across Mary—met my fate, as you might say. But not till he was dead. I called on old Mrs. Wilson when I heard of his death to express my sympathy.

PIPERS AND A DANCER

I think the old lady appreciated it. And I was very much struck with Mary from the first—love at first sight, you might say. She was so plucky—she'd adored Victor, of course—her favourite brother—but I never saw her break down. She went right on working—rolling bandages or something—looking so pretty in her Red Cross kit—but she didn't neglect her mother for all that—regular little housewife—none of this gadding off in trousers to drive lorries in France like so many women. I always say it was the trousers that attracted 'em. That reminds me, we've got too many men coming to-day, only eight ladies. A lot of the men'll have to take the part of ladies. I don't think that'll make much odds, do you? May make a little bit of extra fun, don't you think? "

" Very probably," replied Rodd, starting to attention, for he had been reconstructing Ipsie. " Men would use them for collar-buttons and women for violets—those prize vases, I mean."

PIPERS AND A DANCER

"They ought to be coming," said Heming uneasily, jerking the curtain back. "It's very late."

"Miss Wilson's an artist, isn't she? What do you think of her work?"

"Oh, work's too big a word," laughed Heming. "She can't do anything in colours at all—she only does little things in pen and ink or scratched on wood. Once when she went up to Scotland I asked her to send me a little picture of my native heath, as you might say. She sent me a thing that a child of ten in a Glasgow Board School could have improved on. No drawing in it at all—just lumps in the background for cattle—nothing to show it was heath on the mountains. Her drawing is a nice quiet amusement for her, but she hasn't got any real talent, as you might say. What Mary wants is what most nice young ladies want—to have a good husband who'll look after her, and to have a home and kiddies and chatter to the neighbours about aches and pains as all the ladies do."

Rodd thought, " Very well then, very well—commit bigamy if you like—it's your funeral. For this is what it comes to; you're going to marry two women, the one who came to China last week and the one you remember. Only, if you monopolise your Mary I'm at liberty to think about Ipsie. I want to know where Ipsie gets on."

The room seemed to him so full of the two—Ipsie and Mary—that he could not find space in it for the twenty-four threatened whist players.

" Where is your party? " he asked presently. " That clock still says a quarter of five. It must be mistaken, first or last, but of course it won't admit it. Clocks never do."

" It's stopped," said Heming. He went into the next room and came back at once. " It's half-past six. They were asked at four. Nobody's coming."

The bubble was pricked. The room, just now so full of potential chatter and the

59

ghostly patter of cards, suddenly declared itself silent.

" The weather discouraged them," said Rodd, looking hopefully out at the cloud which was just disentangling its retreating tail from an early star. " It looked all this while as if it might rain any minute."

" No, a deliberate slight," said Heming in a very low voice. " I half expected it. Well . . . I give up now."

They watched the boy, who had a sneer on his face, clear away the card-tables.

During dinner neither spoke. Rodd was trying to reconcile resentment against Heming's neighbours with a vague plan of cabling to Ipsie, " Marriage between you and Jacob unthinkable. Flee at once."

Finally Heming said, " It takes as much courage to bear a thing of this kind as it does to face bullets in the war. And it's a kind of courage I haven't got." He stood up abruptly and left the room. Rodd, to his own surprise, was left with a new thought about the man.

CHAPTER V

IPSIE was late for breakfast. She had been lying in bed remembering all the flatteries of the night before. There had been a dinner-party in honour of Ipsie, not quite perfect but nearly. Pauline had commanded her four most faithful friends to come and add a discreet chorus to her solo in praise of her little sister. In return for a rather good dinner, Masterman Earle had made, in the manner of a wise man, a silly speech in which Ipsie's name stood second only to Pauline's. Christina, the inscrutable stout mistress of Earle, had told Pauline in a detached voice that Ipsie looked like a little fresh daffodil straight from home. Mrs. Hinds had assured Ipsie that any one whom Pauline loved was sure of friends in Hongkong. Captain Norman, who was an economical wit, twice called himself a thorn between two roses. Pauline several times referred to Ipsie with rhetorical ambiguity as a genius, but, to Ipsie's regret, did not specify the nature of her art or refer to her success in *Paint*. However, Pauline's friends were very obedient, and Ipsie, who had never experienced much limelight, except upon her secret stage, was not very discriminating in flattery. She told herself that Masterman Earle had, to all intents and purposes, offered to paint her. In his sneering emphatic voice he had told Pauline, " I'm going straight home to paint you—a red-and-gold-chrysanthemum you—against that peacock screen." And Pauline had laughed and said, " Very well, on condition that you paint my little white-and-silver-anemone sister with her head on my shoulder." " Ah, perfect, perfect," mouthed Masterman.

Pauline had come late and kissed Ipsie in bed, saying, " Dearest, you were the success of the evening."

PIPERS AND A DANCER

And now another flattering day was before Ipsie, and here was Pauline again, glowing with benevolence. The kiss this time implied that breakfast had been waiting for some time. Ipsie was anxiously powdering her nose.

"Ah, little sister, little sister—powder? Whenever I see face-powder I think of the old-world expression—powdered menials."

"Whenever I see it," retorted Ipsie. pertly, "I think of the new-world expression —the veneer of civilisation."

Criticism from Pauline made Ipsie feel as if she had asked for bread and been given a stone.

"The child shows wit," exclaimed Pauline, hugging Ipsie voluminously. "And before breakfast too. Come, little witty one, and have breakfast in front of the pride of my household—a real English fire on an open hearth. It isn't in the least necessary at this time of year, but the mornings are cool and I thought it would make you feel at home."

The real English fire, newly lighted, spat

63

and protested in a real English way. The lumps of coal were as yet like Shadrach, Meshach and Abednego, unscathed in a fiery furnace of wood.

"A letter from Jacob, of course. He insists on addressing you as Mary. A man must have his own special name for his beloved. No man wants to share. . . . But to me you will always be Ipsie—little Ipsie."

"I feel more like Ipsie than Mary," said Ipsie, rather stiffly. "And you make me feel like little Ipsie, Pauline dear."

"I wonder if you will find Jacob changed," mused Pauline. "It seems to me he is changed. He is deeper, more serious, since he had to live in remote lands far from his own kind. Men are tested by solitude, as gold is tested in the fire."

"I hope he hasn't become very deep," said Ipsie. "One of his charms was that he wasn't very deep though he was always serious. It always seemed to me he was a rock of a man—rock of ages cleft for me—

but even when cleft obviously rock right
through. Not—like other wilder rocks—
full of caves and crabs and entombed toads
and little flaws. Jacob would be solid
whether I was glad or sad or mad or bad.
. . . That's why one wants to marry him."

She said *one*, absurdly, because she could
not say *I* without feeling ridiculous and in-
sincere. She wanted very much indeed to
be a married woman. But in a world which
probably contained thousands of beautiful
Captain Normans — why marry Jacob
Heming? Because Jacob Heming offered
her, as solid man to solid woman, marriage
and a footing in the world. Because there
was no one like Conrad in the world. Because
she could not pretend, even to herself, that
any man but Jacob loved her. Oh love—
what a shy and cynical word. . . . She was
suddenly captured by a picture of Jacob
with a broken heart. Ipsie can break a
man's heart. You might meet a man
running, running through sloping rain.
" Can you tell me the way to Glasgow? "

"Don't stop me, don't stop me, I am running away from my broken heart. . . ." Heart of ages, cleft for me. . . . Ipsie had again her old impulse of affection for Jacob because he was so large and full of puzzled effort and because he was so seriously on his own side.

"Solid, yes," said Pauline. "If you mean in sympathy with deep feeling. Deep calling unto deep. But he is a man of high ideals and dignity—he would not be sympathetic to childish moods. You must limit your madness and badness and gladness, dear little sister."

Moods. . . . Moods. . . . Ipsie found nothing in herself but moods. "Pauline," she said, "the more I think of myself the more I hate myself. I wonder if everybody—you—Captain Norman—Jacob—sees how contemptible I am."

"We've all noticed it, darling," smiled Pauline. Her playfulness was overmagnified by her voice and manner. "Especially your new old sister Pauline. For you realise, don't you, that you've

66

trespassed on Pauline's plans for Jacob. Naughty, naughty, irresistible little Ipsie. I told you yesterday that Sophie Hinds loved Jacob nearly as much as you did."

" Mrs. Hinds! Is she a widow? But she's so old."

" She's two years younger than Jacob and five years younger than I am, you silly baby," said Pauline, with a rather laborious smile and caress. " American women often have white or grey hair. Nerves. . . . Life is such a bustle in a young country."

" Was Mrs. Hinds ever really in love with Jacob? " asked Ipsie. She thought, " Even flat-faced women whose glasses are tethered by gold chains to spring buttons on their bosoms have enough love to spare for fat Freemasons who keep their money in purses and suffer from hiccoughs after meals. . . . I oughtn't to think like that of Jacob. I think of him as a husband, not a lover. Husbands, not lovers, may have indigestion. I think of love vulgarly and trivially. It is Conrad's fault—both

67

that I don't know love and that I know I don't know it. The dead Conrad is my conscience now." But this thought posed her brother Conrad in a superior and omniscient pose, watching the triviality of the living Ipsie. The thought was false. Conrad was not her watcher but herself, not a reproach but a glory.

Pauline was silent for a little while before answering Ipsie's question. "I'll admit to you," she said at last, "that to me at one time my brother and Sophie seemed made for each other. I have always been enormously attracted to Sophie Hinds. I don't know why women's women should always be despised and men's men admired. Sophie is a woman's woman. Perhaps I am too. If so I am proud of it. Sophie—you mustn't think I'm making odious comparisons, dear little sister—Sophie could never hate herself and never love herself. Sometimes I think there are two kinds of people— the autobiographists and the biographists. Sophie is a biographist."

PIPERS AND A DANCER

Ipsie thought, " Yes, she would be. Only rather strange people are autobiographists." She matched " Made for each other " with " An artist to her finger-tips." Much of Pauline's conversation seemed to be spoken in inverted commas.

Pauline went on, " She hasn't the heartlessness of the artist "—(" Not .to every finger-tip then," thought Ipsie. " Achilles' finger-tip. . . .") " To me above all she has shown herself." Pauline wanted to make the thing clear. If Sophie was a biographist, Pauline's must be understood to be the principal biography. " I have seen her cry because a ricksha man was insolent to me. Once when we went to the cinema she found that I had no wrap with me, and, before I knew, she was gone to get it—and missed two reels of the picture."

All this left Ipsie a little cold though her Showman was careful to maintain in her face the sweet burning expression of one who discusses a love-affair. " And what about Jacob? " she asked.

69

PIPERS AND A DANCER

" Well, first I must confess. . . . Every woman is born a match-maker, I suppose. Every woman who has decided not to marry is a potential godmother to unborn babies. So I'll be quite frank with you, Ipsie mine, and tell you that Jacob and Sophie had no notion of marrying at first. It was I that willed it and, at first, only I. I am a domineering old sister to Jacob. I set my heart on it when first he came out to China. He and Sophie were to marry, I planned, and I was to introduce him to a good position in Peking with the brother of the head of my firm. Yes, it was my plan—at first. But—well—you'll guess from what I've told you. . . . Sophie could never be behindhand in a matter of love. She is a spendthrift of love and she was not slow to lavish her capital on Jacob. . . ."

The thing seemed to Ipsie grotesque. She could see Sophie Hinds sharply and Jacob only a little more dimly. Mrs. Hinds, tremulous, boneless, brisk; Jacob, heavy, slow, his broad chest and large stomach giving him an imposing upstanding look. It was the kind of couple one connects with a matrimonial agency. Where could Ipsie's Showman pose Ipsie in this respectable parlour drama? Ipsie felt grandly and immensely distant. She saw herself climbing up the long slate-green waves of a great swelling sea in a little boat, and, in the boat, looking up the wave, was Conrad. There was a little ridge of troubled milky water at the crest of the long wave, like broken glass on the top of a wall. Foam slapped Ipsie's face. Between her blinkings she saw a big steamer all awry in the swell, quite close, not more than three long waves away. Thin irregular beads of smoke were strung from her funnels on the wind over the fading orange sky. Looked at through wet eyes the ship seemed to dart forth straight tentacles of light from her yellow port-holes. Dressing for dinner. They're dressing for dinner . . . all we first-class passengers have got smoking-jackets, you see, so there. Jacob's evening cuff-links were green enamelled four-leaved clovers. Sophie, my dear, have you seen my green enamel cuff-links? . . .

" So how did Jacob feel about it? " asked Ipsie. Her vision had made her tremble, yet she felt impelled to escape from the vision back to the silly story of fat Jacob's romance with withered Sophie.

But there, though she did not realise it for a minute, the whole story of Jacob and Sophie broke down. Even Pauline felt that a chasm was opening at the feet of her story. She could not throw a glamorous light on Jacob's side of the matter. His answer to her hint—" Really, Pauline, are you mad? " —had been too uncompromising. She felt again her anger on finding that the sub-ordinate Jacob—with whom she had always been so patient—could silence her, could, in a few vulgar words, finally condemn something of Pauline's choice—almost of her creation. She felt again the exasperating check on her authority, the sensation of uncontrollable spite. " Very well then,

Jacob, very well. . . . No Peking for you if I can prevent it. If you insult my friend you insult me. Get a job for yourself then— you can't expect me to help you."

The broken thread of her story dangled in the air.

" Perhaps Jacob had already the image of his little Ipsie Mary in his eyes," said Pauline. " At any rate Sophie as a lover would have made most people feel inadequate. She has the same effect on me sometimes."

Ipsie thought, " Dear Jacob. Fine Jacob. He could be trusted to make a subtle choice after all. Jacob and Sophie indeed! A mere woman's woman trying to win Ipsie's man. . . ."

" Don't you think," said Ipsie, " that perhaps Mrs. Hinds thought marrying Jacob was the nearest she could get to marrying you, Pauline? "

Then Pauline knew definitely that she disliked Ipsie. She found her elusive and cynical, an outsider coming from a very cold world. She had not hoped to make a friend of Ipsie but experience had justified her in hoping to make a worshipper of her. Ipsie refused to worship; she was—in a word—cynical. It was detestable that Jacob, Pauline's property, should consider marriage with a woman who did not owe allegiance to Pauline. Pauline, who did not impress men, considered it her right to possess all women. She disliked the institution of marriage. She was fond of telling women that she made a god of friendship and that, to such a god, sex played the part of devil.

When Pauline realised that she disliked Ipsie she checked herself and patted her future sister-in-law's hand. This she did, not in hypocrisy but because she was a very conscientious and proud woman who thought often, " I must be fair. I must not allow myself to be influenced by unworthy motives or hasty judgements." She did not of course realise that she also thought, " If I treat her lovingly she will in the end—cease to be cynical." Then there would be no just impediment to Jacob's marriage with her.

PIPERS AND A DANCER

"Darling," she said gently. "You talk of things you don't know about." She changed her voice brightly. "Now, I was forgetting—who do you think telephoned this morning while a little childie I know was still finishing her beauty sleep? Who but Pennell Norman, full of the charms of our Ipsie. I have to go and do some tiresome business this afternoon and Pennell wants to take you for a drive in his car and tea at Repulse Bay. Do you think Jacob would be jealous?"

"I hope so," said Ipsie, at once feeling very gay as she remembered Captain Norman's charming rough eyebrows and brown three-cornered eyes.

"Hongkong, of course, is a vulgar commercial centre," said Pauline playfully. "And you are staying with a vulgar commercial woman. But still I want you not to overlook our virtues—Hongkong's and mine. Hongkong has beauties that stay at home while her business influence travels abroad. My little Ipsie shall bathe in Hongkong's

75

beauty this afternoon and perhaps come home and see more clearly that her old Pauline wishes her well too. . . ."

It was the moment for a kiss and Ipsie, in her new-found graciousness, gave it. Her Showman had her ticketed as *Everybody Loves Her*.

Pauline, though she talked a great deal about beauty, seldom looked about her, except in well-advertised scenery or picture galleries. She had a harsh broad mind and did not readily dislike, tolerate or rejoice in little things. Pauline spent her life in trying to have interesting thoughts in order to conceal from herself something that she unconsciously feared to discover—the fact that she was not a very interesting person. She thought often, " Right living is the highest art of all," and in this way she comforted herself—even praised herself— for her lack of inspiration. She would not admit to herself that only her inferiors admired her art of right living. She was full of a strong pride and refused to regret

that men very rarely sat at her feet and that
women were her adorers, never her friends.

Ipsie read Jacob's letter.

"*My own wee Mary. This is only to bid
you welcome to Hongkong. I am coming down
in ten days and have a great deal to tell you,
but as you know, dear, I am a poor hand with
the pen. I am expecting my successor, Innes,
here any day now. He may have come over
in the same ship as you did. I shall be very
glad to leave Yueh Lai Chou. The people
here are all snobs of the worst kind and as
stingy as mules. I shall have some stories
to tell you that you'll hardly believe. I have
an offer of a position in Shanghai and shall
probably accept it. A man of my standing
and qualifications ought to get something better
but China's not the country it was. The
manager in Shanghai is poor Victor's friend,
Morcambe Breay. In Shanghai we could
make a dear little home and you would like
the life, plenty of neighbours and some good
cinemas. We could make believe we were at
home in a civilised country.*

PIPERS AND A DANCER

There was only one picture for Ipsie in
the letter and that was "My own wee
Mary." A little busy wee wifie, sleeves
rolled up, deft womanly touches ordering
disorder. . . . Where was Ipsie who held
half the wild world behind her eyes? Ipsie's
here, Ipsie's here—it's wee Mary that's
missing. The ghost of wee Mary, wringing
her hands, runs among mountains seeking
a home. She has dropped her duster . . .
the flowers are all tousled in the rough sunlight. Ipsie was frightened by the picture.
"Never mind, never mind . . ." she im-
plored herself. "It's a great mistake but the
great mistakes pass—only little things live
and last. I shall be an anchored woman
called Mrs. Jacob Heming; I shall have a
neat store-room; I shall have babies; I shall
not die alone. If I can't have love I shall
have knowledge. Years don't matter; only
days matter. The loveliness of days cannot
torture or bewilder an anchored woman . . ."

Captain Norman came for Ipsie five
minutes before the arranged time.

PIPERS AND A DANCER

"I'll give you a lesson in driving my little bus," he said. "It's too soon after tiffin for any other cars to be about."

Ipsie as she stepped into the little bus would have preferred to look about her. The singing of the bells of the cathedral followed them as they started and the sound was like the look of the thin golden hills—veiled and remote. The sunlight on the hills was like a smile in eyes not easily amused. The far sea, on which blue clouds and blue and golden islands lay, seemed burnt by a fire of sun and mystery. The junks had red, ribbed sails, high sterns and bows thrust into the water. It seemed that the junks might slant themselves only a little more and slide beneath the water; the islands and the clouds might shimmer beyond bearing and dissolve into the glassy sunlight, and so the devouring sea would be left empty, agape for other prey. But the near sea was kind and intimate. On the little beaches the low tinkling waves broke as sweetly as they break upon the

79

sand-castles of fat-behinded babies in bathing
drawers at Ramsgate.

Ipsie put on the face of her clever eldest
brother Victor as she took the wheel of the
little car. All her life she had had this
habit of half-consciously assuming a sort
of shadow of the look of one or another
of her brothers as her mood changed. She
imitated Conrad most rarely because the
natural Ipsie included so much of the
natural Conrad that imitation was difficult.
When she was trying to be efficient or
practical she raised her eyebrows a little
and scornfully moved her chin from side
to side in the manner of Victor. When she
wished to seem pensive or interesting she
donned the Philip face, protruding her
underlip and half shutting her eyes sullenly.

It seemed after all quite easy to drive a
car, as easy as a new gift is in dreams.
Driving cars was an art that she had always
supposed was confined to the Victors of
the world, people with broad scarred fingers
and dreamless and exact minds. Yet it

was just a habit of the hands, after all, like drawing. She wished the horn would change its note; even the delicate note of the sea was strung on the note of the horn. Ipsie was devouring the writhing road. She had a new power; life and death were in her hands. Even the sun was moving backwards. Get thee behind me, sun.

Victor, who had spent the whole of a legacy on a big white thoroughbred two-seater with a heavy muzzle and solid wheels, used to laugh at the little tame Rovers like this one, owned by penniless subalterns and hopeful younger sons. He called them governess cars. Was her new noble art of driving then a pretence after all, like the old games with chessmen at which also Victor used to laugh? The procession of chariots drawn by leaden dogs and driven by pawns with red silk round their necks had been to her and to Conrad an ecstatic pretence as it clattered through the streets of chessmen towns. It was the better for being a pretence. Real things—expensive

81   G

wax dolls and electric models and dinners at the Ritz and diamonds and helpful friends were limited by their reality; they were just themselves. But little tin two-seaters and dogs and chessmen and chipped wooden bricks and possible romances that came to nothing were everything because they were nothing.

"I'm just a pretence myself," thought Ipsie. "But Pauline is real and she has only probable possibilities."

Captain Norman leaned over Ipsie, a careful hairy hand hovering over Ipsie's hands and the wheel like a mother-bird over her nest.

"You're picking up the idea wonderfully," he said. "I expect you're awfully good at everything, aren't you? Miss Heming says you're a genius."

"I'm an artist, more or less," said Ipsie.

"And not a bit cocky about it either," persisted Captain Norman, speaking aside to the sea in almost as self-congratulatory a voice as if he had created her himself.

"You're so different from the ordinary girls here—they're so damn perky. They paint up and black their eyes and put on no end of side but all the time they're never off their mothers' apron - strings. I should call you a woman of the world, although I don't suppose you're more than twenty."

"By Jove," thought the astonished Ipsie. "I must make a point in future of calling every man I meet beautiful in his hearing by mistake." Her Showman had had his job taken out of his hands. Ipsie was so unaccustomed to flattery that she was un-certain whether Captain Norman's next words would be, "Fly with me." In this case, should she fly?

"I'm twenty-four," she said, beaming foolishly.

They were both silenced by a rather curly stretch of road. Then Captain Norman said, "I met Heming, your fiancé, at his sister's eighteen months ago when he passed through here."

PIPERS AND A DANCER

" Isn't he a dear," said Ipsie in the voice
of a woman of the world.

Captain Norman looked at her for a
moment and then said, " I wonder if you'd
snub me if I said that—well, it's amazing
the men nice girls will marry."

Ipsie's Showman saw his way clear again.
She drew herself up and looked severely at
the road in front.   " Yes, of course I should
snub you if you said that.   I wouldn't say
it if I were you.   You don't know Jacob or
me or the circumstances well enough."

" I've said the wrong thing as usual."

" You didn't say it.   You only asked
what would happen *if* you should say it."

" You are a good sport."

Ipsie was very much pleased with herself.
It seemed to her that she had been both loyal
to Jacob and charming to Norman and she
put on an expression to suit this fortunate
combination.   The only drawback was that
she was going to marry Jacob and would
have to be loyal without applause in future.

All the time she knew that this Good

Sport, this gifted bright woman of the world was as alien to Ipsie as was Heming's own wee Mary.

They had a quiet tea at Repulse Bay, Captain Norman and Good Sport Ipsie and the Showman. They were so early that by the time the band settled down and a crowd of people arrived anxious to dance, Ipsie and her friend were long past the tea stage and their dancing was inspired by a mild cocktail. Their drive home owed its excitement to the inspiration of a second mild cocktail.

A great cloud had walled up the sunset alive. The night was blown with the cloud across the glowing sky.

Captain Norman stopped the car at the side of the deserted road.

" You queer pretty little thing," he said. " I don't believe you care a damn for this man Heming."

Ipsie heard herself saying, " No, I don't care a damn for him."

Captain Norman put his arm round her and kissed her ear. Ipsie did not care a

damn for Captain Norman. But she was
very much flattered by his kiss.

"Then why marry him?" asked Captain
Norman.

Ipsie did not answer though her mind
was full of answers. She did not look round
into Norman's face because she was pretending that another face was close to hers.
"Then there is such a thing as love, after
all," she thought, deliberately hiding the
handsome tiresome sickening face of Norman
from her mind. Perfection's face was close
to hers and now she was Woman, not Ipsie,
never Ipsie again. She had been turned
into a Beloved; she was Manon Lescaut,
Héloïse . . . beloved women might change;
it was only lovers whose faces might not
change. Must she look round, must she
look round and find herself alone with the
long neat mouthing face of Norman? Ah,
Conrad, Conrad . . .

She suddenly found the situation absurd.
She felt as if she had been fed for hours on
emotional sugar. She would feel cleaner

when she should have forgotten this afternoon. Lovers, indeed . . . there were no
lovers; there were Jacobs whom one married
and Normans whom — thank God — one
didn't. Being kissed on the ear by stupid
hairy strangers was the kind of thing that
did not happen to fine sure women. It must
be forgotten at once. How comforting!
Everything can be forgotten in time.

Fortunately it began to rain.

" Oh damn, it's raining," said Captain
Norman, sitting up. " It has no business to
rain at this time of year."

He put up the hood of the car. " It leaks
a bit," he said. " So we'd better push on
before the rain gets worse."

The dim road seemed beaten flat by the
hammers of the rain. The lights of the
harbour stood on the tall stilts of their own
reflections. The rain on the car's wind-
shield splintered and multiplied the lights.
A scrawled distorted sketch of a street could
now be seen through the streaked wet glass.
Umbrellas loomed like polished black moons

through the thick rain. The coolies, shuffling through the dazzle, wore big varnished straw hats sloped forward against the rain. The noise of the rain hissed above the clang of trams and the throb of the car as the noise of the mechanism of a cheap gramophone surges over the drowned echo of Sousa's band.

"How can I quickly take the taste of to-day out of my mouth? Why did to-day come to interrupt my pleasure in myself? Because I have a tiny perception of chastity . . ."

As the car climbed the shining road Ipsie caught a glimpse of Norman's intent and satisfactory face. Pauline's high lighted windows were in sight and here was a flat ending to an artificial experience. Ipsie thought with instinctive disappointment, "He didn't even offer to seduce me," and interrupted herself, "Oh, my God, my God, where am I? Where is my dear self?"

CHAPTER VI

JACOB HEMING rode slowly along the broken paved road out of Yueh Lai Chou. Bubbles of cloud were blown from peak to peak of the mountains and the shadows of the clouds, like blushes of pleasure, suffused the valley's sensitive face.

Riding was Heming's only form of exercise; it was done more from a sense of duty than with any expectation of pleasure. He had a real and serious sense of duty. The two duties he most respected were the duty of not getting too fat and the duty of being a patriotic Englishman. As an Englishman he had always dutifully loved the King and hated the King's Government. He believed that labour members, Irish Catholics, pacifists and those who were not imperialists should be stood against a wall and shot. Yet he boasted of the fact that this step was not taken, on the grounds that it proved the Englishman's love of fair play. It was to him a constant source of grievance that the French neighbours at Yueh Lai Chou could not be induced to admit British superiority. If they would only have admitted it he himself would have been the soul of tact. " Well, this Ong-tongte Cordial makes us all one family, anyway," he would have said and he would have been careful not to dwell more than necessary on the French inferiority, once it was established. Heming of course called the French occupation of the Ruhr, " keeping faith with our lads who died in the Great War," and therefore the lack of active British support often irritated him to the point of gritting his teeth. Yet French criticism of British inaction annoyed him even more. He was nationally sensitive, nationally introspective rather than person-ally so. Like all very patriotic English-men, he never patted poor England on the back. England could do no right in his eyes.

PIPERS AND A DANCER

But nothing ever was right in his eyes. His eyes and his heart were haunted by the ghosts of wrongs and slights, of threats and impossibilities.

On this last ride he travelled, as always, with ghosts. The ghosts crowded out of his world the mountains, the dark compact trees and the dazzling ricefields.

Almost every one Jacob had ever met haunted him cruelly. His mind was an incessant tangle of " He ought to have known. . . . What did she take me for. . . . 'Tisn't as if I. . . . A man of my standing. . . . Speaking as if I was his servant. . . . I simply said to him, perfectly reasonably . . ." All the world, it seemed to Heming, spoke to him and had spoken to him always in an insulting voice. And through the thunders of these changing remembered voices he could always hear his own voice replying reasonably, gently, never insisting on anything but bare rights.

Ipsie haunted him more kindly than did most of the more virile ghosts. For this reason Heming thought very little of Ipsie. She was a good homely little body and he had no doubt that she would, when properly trained, make a good little wife. In his own eyes he was a mild and unpretentious man and his ideas of marriage were utterly unpretentious. Poor Ipsie was partly responsible for the indulgent contempt he felt for her. Clutching desperately and humbly at intimacies that always eluded her, she had asked too much of him at first, built bridges for him, bridges that he would never wish to cross.

"We ought to know each other . . . we ought to know each other better. . . . I am throwing away my pride in writing to you of this. . . . I am telling you this and this and this—you must tell me. . . . Dearest Jacob, we mustn't be strangers to each other. . . ." For several months after they had become engaged the sight of her handwriting on an envelope was tiring to Jacob. He could hear in his head now the voices of those letters, demanding, demanding. . . . He congratulated himself on the patience he had shewn, but still Ipsie's voice joined in chorus with the other grievances in his resonant memory.

" Such nonsense," he thought. " I simply don't know what girls are coming to nowadays. Hysterical I call it. Why, we might be the first couple that ever thought of getting married. Such a fuss. She ought to be glad to get a good solid man these days when so many girls have got to be old maids."

He remembered the love-letters of his father and mother that came into his hands when they died. They knew each other all in good time without all that fuss before marriage. But the ghost of his father, being summoned, must play his full part now. "Stingy as a mule, the old man, right up to the end," thought Jacob, gritting his teeth together. " A man with a son like me, steady, keen on his job, bound to get on—and there was the old man, never a word of encouragement, never a cent after I was twenty, never asked my advice about his rotten investments, and then at the end—

93

nothing—all muddled away in South American gambles—not even enough to support his widow—oh no—shifts all the responsibility of that on to his son who never cost him a penny. . . . And then the old lady . . . just when a man was of an age to marry and found a family—there was the old lady whining for a house of her own in Glasgow. She must have known all along she had cancer but—oh no, not a word about it to me, slaving and pinching away building for her— and did she live to enjoy the house? Oh no, not a bit of it. And it isn't as if she hadn't known all along. House property in Glasgow no sort of investment for a man in China —look at the tenants now—look at the rates. . . ."

Some people set themselves new problems every day but Jacob Heming's problems were as endless and as repetitive as recurring decimals.

The naked and strange mountains swept up round him to the sky. They might have been an enormous wave gathering its forces

94

to break upon him and crush his echoing and solitary world of resentment. But to him the mountains themselves were ghosts. When he looked at their shadow-wrought peaks that stabbed the flying clouds he thought, " Look at me, a man of twenty-two years' experience—isolated in a God-forsaken place like this—no room for enterprise . . . and all simply because the firms in China are too rotten themselves to know a straight man when they see him. I might have been in Peking if Pauline hadn't gone and lost her silly temper just on the one occasion when she might have made her influential friends useful. . . . It wasn't dignified, the way I had to jump at a position like this. And does the Company realise it's got a good man here at last? Not a bit of it, nag—nag—nag—, *keep on good terms with the French and Chinese officials* . . . well, all I can say is, I'd like to see the Prince of Wales himself tackle this Chink magistrate. And the French neighbours—my God. . . ."

He thought of the French Consul, a short

broad young man with a soft rudimentary beard—(so un-English). The French Consul on meeting a man looked at him in polite surprise for about twenty seconds before shaking the hand which had been all this time waiting in mid-air. He was an excessively polite man, the Consul, but when Heming called on him not even a cup of tea was offered—so Heming hated the Consul. There was Dubois, the assistant at the French bank, a fair enthusiastic man who used a great deal of scent and claimed frankly that when he walked among women he walked to the tune of the clink of broken hearts. Dubois had a wife who sang in a small voice from a large bosom—a mountain delivered of a mouse. She sang only Italian operatic music and precariously reached the end of each phrase with a too obvious gasp of surprise and satisfaction. The Dubois gave musical parties at which Heming was never invited to sing. Also they never offered anything but plain water with whisky. Rank outsiders, Heming called them. Then there was Latrille, the agent, who smoked opium and had married an Annamite woman. Heming hated him because of his ivory-yellow family. " Dragging the name of European in the dust," he snorted, though he thought nothing of Europeans. " Rotten colonists, the French. The worst in the world. Of course nobody but the English can colonise."

Heming honestly reviewed his own character again, seeking some explanation of the behaviour of the French neighbours towards him—some explanation of the behaviour of God towards him. He seemed to himself to be an excellent fellow, only too ready to take his part in any clean fun, a ladies' man, no vices. There was, he felt, nothing to dislike in him. All the neighbours at Yueh Lai Chou were, he was convinced, his inferiors, mentally, morally and physically—especially the French. Look at that little tick Fontanet, the railway man, puny, badly dressed, no doubt morally and theologically unsound—yet every one fawned on him, every one laughed and clapped whenever he opened his mouth. " 'Tisn't as if I hadn't got a sense of the ludicrous myself," said Heming. " I can see the funny side as quick as any one. I tell that tale about Maidie in Panama uncommonly well. It made even that conceited puppy Innes laugh."

Rodd Innes had said to himself, " Laugh, laugh. That adventure was delightful to him. Made him feel like a grown man. He has so few delightful things to remember."

The thought of Rodd's laughter over the Maidie yarn was too pleasant to remain more than a few seconds in Heming's memory. The echo of that success died at once as he attuned his ears again to the accustomed haunting voices.

The mountains edged nearer to the road; the valley narrowed and climbed. Heming had passed through the last little town among the rice-fields; he was above rice-fields now. On either side, quick rocky slopes sprang up; between the rocks, yellow lilies and big blue harebells nodded in the rank and colourless grass. The tall pale grasses, catching the

98

sun, made a frosty bloom, almost like grape-bloom, over the dark westward slopes. The road climbed to a horned gateway which stood high against the sky just where the springing gorge was narrowest. Beyond the gateway there was a new world—a world of thin pine-trees and red shouting streams, and villages tenderly striped with the shadows of trees that in the springtime blazed with apricot blossom or pomegranate.

Heming rode on with his eyes on his pony's mane. The tiny mountain tribes-women passed in a swirl of kilts and tassels, their turbaned snakelike hair bound high with silver and scarlet cords. Caravans passed him in a long clatter of hoofs and a clamour of shouts and bells. The foremost mule of each caravan was gay and proud, nodding his head under the nodding benediction of his flag of office—a tall bamboo striped in scarlet and blue like a barber's pole and surmounted by a mop of coloured cotton; attached at a steep angle to his pack, this contrivance must be a beacon to the lesser mules that followed.

PIPERS AND A DANCER

On the last mules or ponies of the caravans rode the noisy drivers, seated very high on the packs, their sandalled feet on the ponies' necks, blue turbaned, tassels swinging on either side of their brown cramped mountain faces, often armed with heavy old rifles, often singing thin endless songs. Jacob Heming hardly looked aside from his pony's mane as these strangers passed. There was no room for singing strangers in his world of detested and indispensable ghosts. He was glad when the road was empty, glad when the birds stopped singing. It seemed suddenly that a mountain lifted its head and Heming's pony waded in a mountain's shadow, a shadow like cool thin water.

" Getting late, I must turn back," he said, wondering a little why he had come out. He remembered that Rodd was paying calls this afternoon. " Probably cadging dinners out of all the people who won't do a hand's turn to show their appreciation of *my* work. All for a new face, that's what they are. By Jove, if he's got himself asked out to dinner these next few days without me being invited, I'll let him have a piece of my mind. 'Tisn't as if I . . ."

Rodd was pleased to be left alone at Yueh Lai Chou. 'He was a superficially cordial and adaptable person, and it was rarely he found people so inaccessible, so fortified in distrust as he found Heming. It was interesting but rather laborious, like living with a person whose language one scarcely knew. Rodd never wanted to make efforts. He was, however, sorry for Heming, and therefore tolerant of him. The thought of Ipsie complicated his feelings very much. The fact that she had decided—surely in ignorance of the facts—to marry Heming acted on Rodd's mind as a nail in the shoe acts on the foot. It wasn't so much the facts that she was ignorant of—it was something more serious, more difficult than facts. He felt himself under a sort of obligation to think much of Ipsie, to have her round pale face often before his eyes. And when he found

that this Ipsie who strayed a little tentatively,
a little plaintively, in and out of his thoughts,
was incredibly remote from the Ipsie who
presided demurely over the domestic section
of Heming's thoughts, he felt curiously free
and triumphant. It seemed that his Ipsie
was his trove; he had a right to her. He
walked about full of pleasure in his Ipsie,
remembering tiny movements in her face,
twists in her soft voice, the tremulous and
shy honesty in her too frequent confessions,
memories and discoveries that were not
Heming's and never would be, though he
might lie down beside the cosy little body of
his wee Mary every night for forty years.

"She won't be content to be a misunderstood wife," thought Rodd. "She never
allows herself to be misunderstood for a
minute. She'll explain. She won't wait
for Heming to break her illusions. She'll
break them herself."

Rather irrelevantly he remembered one of
Ipsie's first remarks to him. After they had
identified each other as Jacob Heming's

future wife and Jacob Heming's successor in business—"Well, we must know each other," Rodd had said. "We'll start by telling each other the stories of our lives." Ipsie's story began, "Since the year eighteen hundred and ninety-nine, I have been a childless spinster." And when she heard him laugh she became red and said, "I ought to tell you—I've made that joke before. . . ." That was her concealing veil—too much explanation of herself, too much confession. That was the influence that had a little chilled Rodd after their first delighted two days of mutual attraction.

But now, contrasting himself with Heming, he felt himself a god of understanding. He felt that Ipsie was a lovely secret thing that he, a god, had made. It was lucky, he thought, all things considered, that he had not fallen in love with her.

He walked about under the gay sun paying the calls that duty obliged him to pay. The French Consul's wife had given him tea and merrily smacked his arm. Dubois had

shown him a wonderful pair of executioners'
swords with wrought silver hilts. Latrille
had some cute little half-caste kiddies. As
for Fontanet, Rodd had nearly injured himself by calling on Fontanet; the man had
made him laugh till his stomach ached. It
wasn't too easy to be a buffoon in a foreign
tongue. But Fontanet had no right to be so
funny—mimicry was rightly considered a low
form of wit in Boston. Only, in that imitation
of the Maidie story as told by Jacob Heming
there was exactly enough of the real story, the
real Jacob voice, the real sentiment, on the
one side, and on the other side exactly enough
of the outrageous mocking Fontanet. Too
bad to laugh though. Rodd laughed again.

He had no pang of shyness and no embarrassing picture of himself when he entered
the houses of strangers. He always expected to be liked, even by English people,
who always seemed to him to be speaking
politely against their own better judgement.
He was quite a vain young man. He frequently spent minutes together in front of a

mirror, not so much looking at his face as happily seeking the Rodd that people obviously liked. It was lucky, he thought, that he could get himself across, such as he was.

He called on the next family on his list, Dr. and Mrs. Marrowby. English, Heming had told him, and as stingy as mules.

Dr. and Mrs. Marrowby and Rodd sat in perfect silence for about two minutes after shaking one another's hands, but Rodd was not embarrassed. This was the English manner, and Rodd found it curiously provocative, but not unfriendly. Silences like this always inspired him to make fantastic remarks that could never have been uttered in the cordial busy atmosphere of an American gathering. At an English luncheon party once, the silence had obliged him to climb to the top of a high flag-pole quite unexpectedly. After hearing himself chew fish for five minutes, Rodd, looking out of the window, had felt impelled to say, " Don't your guests ever want to climb your flag-pole between courses? " The hostess had replied, " Oh, *please* do," and when the fish was finished they all came out rather sadly but conscientiously and watched him do it. The English, as all good Americans knew, had no sense of humour. But this kind of incident gave Rodd an uneasy and exciting feeling he might be on the verge of the discovery of a new England—of the English equivalent of a sense of humour. Remarks that led directly up flag-poles were seldom made in Boston.

⌐Now, in the presence of the Marrowbys, Rodd, having looked round for something, if possible, a little lower than a flag-pole, said, "Doesn't it seem a bit queer to Oscar Wilde to be stalled there between the Bible and Stephen Leacock?"

"It's Donnie," said Mrs. Marrowby proudly. "Our boy who's just left school. He arranges the books by their size and not by their sense. We are so glad you've come. Somebody young for Donnie."

"You must come to dinner," said Dr. Marrowby. "What about to - morrow night?"

" To-morrow night. . . . Heming 'll still be here. He's not leaving till Friday."

" H-m-m-m." . . . They obviously did not want to ask Heming.

" He came here last week without being asked," said Dr. Marrowby. " Said he'd come to watch us play bridge. The bridge finished and still he wouldn't go. It was eight o'clock. My wife went away to dress. I said to Heming at last—'Well, dinner-time, I suppose. Where are you dining?' He said, ' I don't know.' At a quarter to nine my wife sent in the boy to tell me dinner was ready. I said, ' Well, this isn't good-bye, I suppose—we shall see you again before you go . . .' and he said, ' Yes—which evening? I have no engagements.' . . ."

" Why, it's this way," said Rodd, rubbing his chin in some agitation, as if he himself had been reproached. " Circumstances someway shew him at his worst here. He's a terribly solitary man. He needs friends . . ."

" No wonder," said Dr. Marrowby, but

PIPERS AND A DANCER

Mrs. Marrowby asked Rodd to bring Heming with him on the next night to dinner.

As Rodd came to Heming's house the shadow of the pagoda seemed to flow over the verandah as the sun went down.

" It's getting late," said Rodd paternally. " It'll be dark soon. Where can the man be?"

Jacob Heming had turned back as the tide of shadow climbed up the valley. There was no sunset colour in the west yet, but in the east a nearly round moon bowled coldly between fiery clouds. The road followed a bend in the gorge, and as Heming came round with the glare of the fiery clouds in his eyes he found himself in the midst of an oncoming group of sixty or seventy men. About one-third of them were mounted, riding high on packs and without reins as Chinese mountain caravan men ride. The rider nearest to Heming had a gong which grumbled as it moved against the pony's shoulder.

Heming's pony, which, like all well-fed Yunnanese ponies, was belligerent—not having been gelded—neighed and kicked as the foremost ponies passed. Heming had some difficulty in controlling it, and it was not till half the passing crowd was behind him that he noticed that the men of the caravan were not anxious to make way for him. Through the senseless screaming of his excited pony he suddenly heard behind him the splintering crash of the gong, and immediately he found himself firmly wedged in the crowd. A man with a large turban seized his bridle. Heming was fascinated by the man's expression ; he could not for a few moments drag his eyes from the face in front of him. The narrow dark eyes of the Chinese, set in protruding pouches, were almost shut ; sweat was pouring down from under his turban ; his mouth was twitching, the upper lip caught up intermittently into a tremulous snarl. This was easy, Heming thought ; the man, insolent though he might be, was terrified. But as Heming lifted his whip to give the man a cut across the face, he looked over his immediate assailant's

head and saw the muzzle of a rifle and behind
it a barrier of gaping faces half dimmed by
the flaring clouds behind them. There was
a bristle of rifles against the light. The blood
thundered in Heming's ears. He could
scarcely breathe. " In a minute I shall
laugh and say, ' Well, that gave me quite a
turn.' It is not possible that these stinking
apes can have got the upper hand over ME."
The man who pointed the rifle at Heming
had an atrocious squint. Heming, acting
before he could calculate, gave his pony a
violent slash and rode straight at the squint-
ing brigand. The sound of rifle-shots seemed
to blow the yellow air to pieces. Heming's
pony, wild with fright, threw its forelegs into
the air, slipped and fell backwards. Heming,
lying on the ground, did not move. He had
a vague idea that the earth was his salvation.
A heavy man with his back to the ground was
a king on his throne, a fugitive in sanctuary.
While his head rang with the shock of his fall
he could hear the echoes of the shots shuttling
up and down across the twilit valley.

CHAPTER VII

PAULINE was not happy unless she was doing some rather exaggerated thing. To-day she was strenuously nursing Ipsie, who had a cough. Ipsie did not feel ill, only to-day she knew all the time that she had a body— eight stone of body to a pennyweight of brain, she said to herself rather querulously.

Ipsie sat in a big chair by the window. A fold of exquisite air enclosed Hongkong. One could hear, it seemed, the humming of the loom on which the spangled fabric of the air was woven. The wind among the shrubs outside sounded very gay. Winds among leaves are always gay ; only in streets the winds sound sorrowful. Ipsie's eyes were full of beautiful things that she remembered, full of flatteries and thoughts of Conrad.

PIPERS AND A DANCER

Her mind was enjoying playtime. She thought of herself as she had seen herself described by an interviewer in the pages of an American woman's paper, an Ipsie with a " keen childlike face under a crown of pale golden hair." It did not describe Ipsie's Ipsie but it published an Ipsie of some kind to the world. Hundreds of readers of that paper must have thought, " How charming she must be . . ." and this thought was delightful to remember. She rejoiced vaguely in the knowledge that she was so acutely sentient. Being lost and having eyes was gloriously exciting. Many people wondered about her though few loved her. That Congressman . . . she thought of herself motoring with a Congressman— surely a history-maker of a kind, surely a member of that class of Interesting Men from whom splendid women's lovers are recruited — motoring with a delightfully polite Congressman from Baltimore to Washington. She was proud of having seen Washington so ideally. Washington under

a veiled sun was a city that all day long
remembered the moonlight. Among dark
trees the Capitol, very white and delicate,
again and again retrieved the escaping sight.
The city was a white web spun to catch
dreams in a sheen of dew. At the centre of
the web crouched the pale spider Capitol
watching its handiwork and waiting for its
prey of dreams. Caught in the snare of
Washington, roaring among fat family cars
along too wide avenues, Ipsie had seen
Washington as a city that could never live up
to its distant promise. The gossamer threads
were called boulevards (with a hard D)—and
had no snare for dreams ; the Capitol had
outgrown its bloom. There were excres-
cences of statuary everywhere ; Ipsie seemed
to remember draped stone ladies with crimped
hair, blowing trumpets. Probably Peace,
but surely not the Peace we fought for. . . .
Poor Washington, democracy brooded like a
hen on the ivory white egg of the Capitol.

" Wherever I go," thought Ipsie, " I find
I have left behind the thing I came to see."

She was proud again because her eyes were so articulate. Would Jacob double or halve the delight of her eyes?

" Pauline, do you think Jacob and I will ever go adventuring? " She thought of herself, Mrs. Heming, gold crowned and childlike, facing wild but stingless adventures in far continents in company with congressmen and kings. " I want to go back to America. . . ." America was a country where all the tattered dreams were left blowing about on street corners with nobody but stray Ipsies to pick them up.

" Jacob's a home-bird," said Pauline. " He'll want his little wife to stay a good deal by the fireside, I know. All good men do. As for the United States, he's never been there and he certainly doesn't want to."

" Pauline, do you think I really ought to marry Jacob? "

Pauline thought, " I mustn't be petty," so she said, " Dear childie, I think you ought to follow the dictates of your own heart."

" I haven't any heart," said Ipsie proudly.

PIPERS AND A DANCER

It was curious, the more warmly Pauline spoke of Jacob, the more impossible Jacob seemed to Ipsie. Ipsie had known Jacob, it seemed to her, well. She had known at least what to expect of him. An incurious safe person standing on firm ground, a person who would hold her hand and steady her on the slippery giddy peak that was herself. But when Pauline spoke of him it was as though she spoke a word outside its ordinary context, a familiar word that had suddenly disclosed an ominous and scarcely known meaning. Would Ipsie die then, married, and would wee Mary live Ipsieless by Jacob's side till Jacob and she were old and blind? Jacob's wee Mary, concealing the fact that she did not exist, following devoutly behind Jacob's broad back in at the doors of orthodox churches and cinema palaces. You can't discover one foot of clay on an idol without suspecting the other.

Ipsie wanted to be saved from Ipsie and yet she could not bear her secret Ipsie to die. Wee Mary would be a poor exhibition for the Showman. Wee Mary was blind to terror and delight. Wee Mary had never known Conrad.

" I shall have *Sic transit gloria mundi* engraved inside my wedding-ring."

Mrs. Sophie Tooloose Hinds and Captain Norman came to tea. Ipsie thought nothing at all about Captain Norman since Pauline had told her that he was married. He was now to her a blank—something that she did not at all understand. Having decided that he was not a wicked seducer of innocent girls nor the romantic victim of an uncontrollable passion for Ipsie Wilson, she was left with no understanding of him at all. He had sharp horse-chestnut coloured eyes and a face that seemed accurately made to match a hard and slender body—that was the end of the story, Ipsie thought. She gasped a little with humiliation when she thought of the beginning of the story, but soon she would be away from him. Intervening space would blot him out.

Mrs. Hinds sat rigidly ready to look

receptive when Pauline should speak. Ipsie, looking at her three friends, was conscious all at once of the little occasion as a queer junction of lives. Trailing their innumerable threads behind them, they four faced one another mysteriously. The threads behind them, joining at the tea-table, spread outward in a net over half the world, secret threads into lost lives, lost places and stories, days and delights and disasters. She imagined their four lives like a map of trade routes, thin lines converging to a knot—the eyes of Ipsie watching at the knot. She imagined cargoes of lives and dreams coming in to the watchful port of Ipsie for a day and leaving soon without unloading—leaving for ever for unknown seas.

" Isn't it a pity that nobody can ever really tell anything," said Ipsie. " How we could all fascinate each other if we could speak."

" How d'you mean? " asked Captain Norman almost before she had finished speaking.

" She means," interpreted Pauline bene-

volently, " that every man is a mystery to his
neighbour. A platitude, dear solemn little
sister."

" Absolutely," agreed Ipsie. " A platitude. A duck-billed platitude. Only I
mean—our lives are full of such splendid and
heart-breaking stories that we never can tell."

A quick flash of story crossed her mind.
It was not hers but Conrad's. It was neither
begun nor ended. Conrad was climbing
from the back of a horse in at the window of
an inn. There was music overflowing the
inn. Conrad jumped from the window-sill
into a room full of music, as a swimmer
springs into moving water. All the men
about the piano were either singing or dancing. They danced stamping dances like
Russians, kicking out their heavy boots from
under their haunches. They danced frantically, but afterwards they sang slow songs
their light young silver voices curving away
from one another in harmonies, as springing
thin lines part in running water. *My lodging
is on the cold ground, And oh, very hard is my*

fare. . . . Ipsie's ears pulsed with the sharp and eccentric harmonies. Conrad held his head a little stiffly, a little to one side, listening sharply, fitting his voice accurately between the curving mazing voices. *I'll twine thee a garland of straw, love. I'll marry thee with a rush ring.* . . . Ipsie was choking with pleasure. . . .

Mrs. Hinds and Norman looked back rather dubiously at their lives. Captain Norman's life was flat and exact like a photograph, and he was not in the least disappointed in it. He had never known ecstasy. He had passed out of Sandhurst half-way down the list. He had married his wife because at the time she seemed to him a Better Sport than she had actually proved to be. The war, during which he had been twice slightly wounded, never caused him a moment's passion, hope or despair. The only stories he ever listened to or passed on dealt with being drunk or kissing girls. He had probably kissed about forty girls since he married, but he was a virtuous young man and often remembered not only his wife but his mother. He believed that his distant admiration for Pauline " did him good." Ipsie was nothing more than rather kissable —not very. His frequent senseless adventures with girls gave him very little satisfaction, but they made him feel somehow that he was fulfilling his duty as a man and a soldier. He had met several thousands of men and women in his life without noticing anything fantastic or suggestive about one— yet, when Ipsie had spoken, he knew dimly for a moment that wonderful stories and unconsidered beauties had indeed brushed his life. There had been voices perhaps. . . . Like a guest at an uncongenial dinner-party who is roused by nothing but his own name, while voices had filled his ears only one word or a few words had power to catch his attention. Those were the only words he knew.

Mrs. Hinds' life was full of stories but she was disastrously selective. She imposed a standard upon dreams, and as the standard was a moral and quasi-literary one the dreams

died before ever they reached it. Mrs.
Hinds looked back to a respectable and
talented childhood in a small town in
Illinois. When she was only fifteen the
Mayor had personally congratulated her on
a poem she had written—it had brought
state-wide credit, he said, on her home-town.
She had married an increasingly inebriate
travelling salesman. Her art and her devotion to two or three women friends had
been her refuge. The refuge had shielded
her not only from sorrow but from life.
When her salesman died she was still spiritually a virgin. Her writing catered pain-
lessly to the painfully ordinary. Through it
she believed that she was helpful to other
stricken women and the stricken readers
believed the same. Pauline Heming had
been a revelation to Mrs. Hinds, for she
was a humble woman. She looked upon
Pauline's flat as a salon; in its atmosphere
her mild axiomatic gift flourished; there too
she had daringly conceived—with Pauline's
help—the idea of inspiring a passion in the

PIPERS AND A DANCER

breast of Jacob Heming. She had long hoped to marry again; she said that she still felt she had something to Give. Certainly she was a woman replete with every modern convenience.

" Wonderful stories need not only a teller but a hearer," she said now, thinking of the letters she frequently received from stricken readers enclosing a two-cent stamp to cover the cost of a sympathy never withheld by Sophie Hinds. Just as a dog pricks its ears for an expected sound, so Mrs. Hinds pricked her pince-nez for Ipsie's reply. Ipsie was trying to imagine that brisk and brittle face melted with love. " Perhaps every one is either a born lover or a born lovee," thought Ipsie. " Except me—I am neither; that is why I am so lost. Sophie Hinds has to be a lover because she's too withered and good to be a lovee."

Pauline's boy brought in a telegram. It was for Ipsie. As Ipsie opened it her Showman did not forget to prepare on her face the expression of a recipient of shocking news.

She read, *Heming captured by brigands.
No immediate cause for anxiety. I will take
all possible steps and keep you informed. Rodd
Innes.*

Brigands . . . brigands. . . . Is it a
joke? . . .

Pauline took the telegram, and even while
she read it she could be seen rising to the
occasion. " Now we must be brave; we
must just think calmly what had best be
done."

She handed the telegram to Mrs. Hinds,
who said, " Oh my, oh my, oh my," and
after taking off her glasses and wiping them
once or twice, suddenly dissolved into tears
with thin high sobs.

While Pauline sat thinking nobly and
calmly she took Ipsie's hand and held it very
firmly.

" She would be adorable if only one adored
her," thought the shaken Ipsie. " She is as
safe as a strong tower. She would be strong
and safe if one were dying."

" At any rate I take it we can't be content

to stay here waiting for news. We will go up to Yueh Lai Chou. It is a perfectly simple journey. The pure mountain air will do my Ipsie's cough good. Probably our dear Jacob will be there waiting to greet us, but if not we can live in his house and be ready to welcome him home."

" Don't leave me behind . . . don't leave me behind . . ." cried Sophie Hinds in a cracked voice.

That Jacob had become "Our Dear Jacob" seemed to all Pauline's hearers very ominous. Captain Norman offered funereally to go and make inquiries about ships to Tonkin.

Ipsie sat imagining the large form of Jacob Heming with square face uptilted and proud eyes downturned, in the manner of the cinema hero at bay; she saw him the centre of a yelling crowd of operatic-looking brigands in black and scarlet. She saw him bound to a tree, his elbows behind him; she saw herself riding at a rattling canter with a party of British cavalry to the rescue. She was able to mock these imaginings quite gaily. To think of Jacob a prisoner gave her violent excitement but no pain. She thought, ." I shall see Rodd again." She thought for a moment soberly and cynically of Rodd and hoped that he would see her picturesquely at last.

CHAPTER VIII

NOBODY in Yunnan except Rodd seemed very much excited about Heming's capture. The further away people were the more notice they seemed to take of it. The northern China and Hongkong newspapers were convulsed; the name of Heming was said to ring like a gong through Peking; probably England talked of intervention in China once and for all. In Yunnan province, however, the consul seemed to consider the matter nothing more than a tiresome increase of his duties. And in Yueh Lai Chou itself, the officials were only surpassed in tranquillity by Heming's neighbours. The paragraph in a Shanghai newspaper describing Heming as a well-known and popular resident of Yunnan was in Yueh Lai Chou strongly resented.

PIPERS AND A DANCER

Dr. Marrowby, a kind man, said, " Well, well . . . poor chap. . . . Someone's pressed him to stay at last. . . ."

Rodd's call on the Chinese magistrate, accompanied by Heming's interpreter and by the peasant who had brought Heming's letter, was a baffling experience. The magistrate, in a mustard-brown silk robe surmounted by a little Eton jacket in black brocade, would speak to Rodd only, it seemed, across unfriendly spaces. The high stiff blackwood chairs, their narrow seats made the more unretentive by slippery red quilted mats, were all ranged against the walls. The magistrate, having bowed Rodd to a chair at one end of the room, himself sat down impassively at the other. It would have taken more courage than Rodd possessed to drag a chair forward to within a chatty American business distance of the official. Rodd felt that if he advanced at all the magistrate might retreat at once to the other end of the compound.

PIPERS AND A DANCER

The magistrate was a sad-looking man with bloated pouches under his eyes and a long thin moustache tucked into the deep creases below his cheeks.

" He sess," remarked the interpreter to Rodd, " that he will examine the matter of Missster Heming'ss capture."

It was with the greatest difficulty that Rodd saved the interview from ending abruptly at this point. Some cups of tea were brought in and the magistrate bowed over his cup in dismissal.

" No, but stop," cried Rodd, choking over his tea. It was very hot and leafy and the bowl was roofed in by another bowl which was difficult to manage. " Tell him that this is a very serious and urgent matter and must be fixed up at once."

" It iss imposssssssible," said the interpreter severely, " to command a high Chinese offisssial."

" Well, put it any way you want. Give him my love if it'll make him feel any better. Tell him that for the honour of his district he needs to have this business cleared up right away."

"He sess," said the interpreter after an almost inaudible exchange of remarks, "that there iss very ssmall number ssoldierss in Yueh Lai Chou at the pressent. Also the General iss away. He sess he will examine the matter. He will quesstion high offisssial at Yunnan-fu."

"But what about the gink who brought the letter from Heming?" persisted Rodd. "Can't he be questioned?"

"He sess he iss ihformed that thiss gink iss ssimple peassant who knowss nothing of the banditss."

Rodd rose and cracked his fingers irritably. The magistrate grew calmer and calmer. He seemed to be receding into ephemeral mists of calm.

"Tell him," said Rodd, "that the British authorities will look on the matter very seriously and that inaction on the part of the Chinese authorities will make a very bad impression. King George will probably hear of it and be very seriously annoyed. Tell him that, as far as I understand, the ransom is very unlikely to be paid—foreign governments don't do bargains with a handful of dirty crooks. The military authorities here will be held responsible for Mr. Heming's safety. Ask him how soon soldiers will be sent."

" He sess," said the interpreter, " that he will examine the matter."

At the gate the interpreter explained to Rodd, " Misster Heming has been offending to thiss offisssial. He hass given him rough unpolite wordss and hass been telling him that he iss thief of electric light. Magistrate hass no haste to sserve Misster Heming."

Rodd rode to the distant main-line to meet Pauline, Ipsie and Mrs. Hinds. He almost danced up and down the station with impatience. The astonished Chinese lingerers on the platform followed him up and down the long untidy station, supposing at each turn that he would do some extraordinary thing that would make their patient pursuit worth while. The vendors of pocked hard-bake, dry sunflower seeds, lumps of dough and flat scarred unleavened cakes, moved their straw trays out of his way to give him a clear path. They all sat on their haunches discussing his hat among themselves and laughing at intervals, for, though perfectly usual in Boston, it seemed to them a very amusing hat.

Pauline, Ipsie and Mrs. Hinds arrived very cross. Travelling with Pauline, Ipsie thought wildly, was like travelling with the Albert Memorial. Pauline was built up of monumental goodness, but nothing seemed fantastic or funny in her presence. In Haiphong, in Hanoi, at wayside stations in Tonkin, as the broad-faced peasants laughed through betel-juice, Ipsie often wondered how they dared—how indeed they could possibly laugh at Pauline. Was there, after all, a funny aspect to that fine benevolent figure? Pauline, her dark dust-cloak thrown back like a queen's ermine, looked proudly and tolerantly from Annamite to Frenchman, from palm to banana, from pig to temple. Ipsie tickled her mind with impossibilities. " If she ever got the giggles . . ." she thought daringly. " She would look so— she would look so——" How could Pauline look? She could look as keen and as splendid as the graven blade of a great sword. Not funnier than that.

Ipsie felt painful and weary all the way from the coast, and for this reason she had not felt very much concerned with the misfortune of Jacob, but had sustained the journey in a condition of dreary tranquillity. This displeased Pauline. Pauline's strong arm was ready to go round a confiding, broken-hearted little Ipsie; but here was a silent impersonal Ipsie, smiling sulkily, an Ipsie to whom " little " seemed no fitting prefix. It was plain that Pauline considered Sophie Hinds by far the more satisfactory lover of the two. Even Mrs. Hinds' shameless train-sickness was subtly exhibited by Pauline to Ipsie as proof of the real lover.

PIPERS AND A DANCER

Mrs. Hinds had completely and disastrously lost her briskness. She had collapsed awry as hopelessly as a starched collar on a hot man's neck. By mourning for the stricken Jacob who was destined for another's arms, Sophie Hinds was living up to a standard which exactly suited her ardent, chaste and edifying instincts. She was married to a great sorrow, and even years hence, as sorrow's widow, she looked forward to wearing uplift and reticent—though well-advertised—courage as her widow's weeds. Her present feelings, of course, were too deep for words—even for well-paid words in an earnest domestic woman's weekly. But she was saving them up in a small diary; she did not mean to waste them. Feelings that are too deep for words can and must acquire a new depth in print, as all American writers for women know.

The traveller intending to arrive at Yueh Lai Chou can either change from the little French main-line on to a still smaller Chinese tin-carrying line, and so, after the sacrifice of many hours and much perspiration, reach the very walls of his destination—or else he can be met by a caravan of ponies, palanquins and pack-horses at a small halt on the main-line and be carried for an hour or so across the valley to Yueh Lai Chou. Every host in Yueh Lai Chou who properly values his approaching guests resorts to the latter scheme, and it was on the ledge in the mountains by the main-line that the feverishly amiable Rodd shook the hands of Pauline, Ipsie and Mrs. Hinds.

Ipsie at once saw a new thing in Rodd's eye and looked forward to falling in love with him within the next twenty-four hours and out of love within a week. She hoped that Rodd was not as defective as herself in the matter of faithfulness. She often played childishly with thoughts of undying passion in others. She wanted to be to several men the limitless and compelling dream that Conrad was to her. She hoped that she might put on that cloak of perfection, but not that any man might ever wear it for her.

PIPERS AND A DANCER

It would be difficult to say why she retained her faith in herself as a possible object of great love—no man had ever loved her with passion and she did not permit herself many illusions, in spite of the influence of the Showman. The Showman perhaps insisted on claiming that he had something to show.

To Rodd, who had been conducting liaisons with various Ipsies of his own and Jacob's creation, this was a new Ipsie standing on the noisy mountain station. She was very white; she wore a threadbare tolerant expression which obviously covered a mood of exasperation; there was a forlorn smut on her nose that somehow made him feel very tender. " Well, that's settled," thought Rodd. " I won't allow her to marry Heming. I'll expose Heming to her." It would be, he realised, very much more difficult to expose Heming behind his back than in his presence. The man stood now high on a pedestal of misfortune. Had he not been so dramatically removed he would have exposed himself. Heming's self was the only accusation; lacking Heming there seemed to be no charge to make—just as, present, Heming would surely have had no defence.

" It only needs a little cleverness," thought Rodd, looking eagerly at the endangered smiling Ipsie. " And cleverness is what I've got."

He was worried by the size of Pauline and by her strenuously loving expression. " Who said that Heming had no defence? " he thought. But it was certain that Ipsie must be saved. Looking at her he remembered with disgust Heming's voice: " 'Tisn't as if . . . Stingy as mules . . . what all nice girls want. . . ."

But on the way to Yueh Lai Chou, Ipsie had more chance to look at Rodd than he to look at her. His pony rocked gently in front of her chair; whenever he turned or looked away up the valley, she could see his short face, his thin square shoulders, the low surprised forehead in the shadow of his hat. But she always laboured under the burden of too intense sight; she knew faces too well even if she did not love them. Her eyes were so indiscriminately greedy that they devoured too much. She knew Rodd's face too well just as she knew too accurately the face of the coolie who had held his pony at the station, the tiring fine face of Pauline, the oblong face of the steward in the ship from Hongkong, the face of Jacob Heming, the face of a water-buffalo on the dike, mutely reproaching her calf for being in the way. Living in her dazzle of things seen and never forgotten, Ipsie was for ever on the precarious verge of lassitude.

There had been a feast in Yueh Lai Chou and all the tribes-people were coming home from the city to the mountains, meeting Rodd's caravan of guests and ponies. The Lo-lo women stood in excited files on the banks to let the travellers pass; they were all in their feasting clothes, in lilacs and faded pinks and gay greens, their bosoms bright with embroidered breast-plates, their backs hunched under the babies strapped in coloured cloths to their shoulders, their winged embroidered sun-bonnets bound about their heads with silver chains. A kilted group went by, their heads encircled by broad leathern bands thickly studded with silver. There were three tiny women in dark blue with a smart touch of scarlet, striped sleeves, sailor collars, big careless dark turbans; their kilts were bunched absurdly behind like bustles under prominent short coat-tails. All along the dwindling far road the tribes-people could be seen coming. The sun was behind them and they twirled their gay scarlet and yellow paper umbrellas on long seven-foot stems against the low following light. It seemed that these shining, spinning golden circles blew like bubbles on a slow wind from the sun.

In the mountains to the south, Rodd had told Ipsie, Jacob Heming had met with the brigands. There seemed to Ipsie to be a chasm between the world of credible happenings and the shocking adventure of Jacob. Jacob seemed to have gone too far from the realm of rational adventures to be very inter-

esting to Ipsie. A picture in her eyes of
Jacob sitting irascibly inert among steep
slopes of wild flowers left her curiously cold.
Yet she thought about him often and told
herself that wild flowers in the light of a
low sun under beetling clouds were all she
had at the moment in common with him.
She thought that a bridge of flowers across a
chasm was perhaps a less ephemeral bond
than the personal bonds between them.

Directly the travellers arrived at the house
beside the lake Rodd showed them a letter
that he had received from Heming.

*Dear Innes—This bloody business is just
like my luck. I dare say if the truth were
known these dirty thieves wouldn't have dared
kidnap a man of my standing without some kind
of* official *backing. I told you there was a
conspiracy against me. Bring pressure to bear
on those devils the officials. I can't tell you
where I am because I don't know. I have been
dragged post haste over practically pathless
country for forty-eight hours, and had lost my
bearings even before we began last night's march*

*which finished me altogether. In the end they
let me ride on the wooden saddle of a pack
mule. For God's sake don't annoy or molest
the scoundrel who brings this letter, but give
him the stores mentioned on the list below.
Your treatment of him is of course reflected
on me.*

*As far as I can understand—(these beasts
don't talk any intelligible jargon)—the ransom
they want is $50,000. Quite apart from any
personal question, British prestige demands that
I should be released at once, even at this price.
Impress on the Consul the national importance of
the capture of* the Manager of a British firm of
high standing. *I should think that he would
see for himself that every day I spend in the
hands of these ruffians is an insult to British
prestige. It is no good relying on a rescue by
Chinese soldiery—too dangerous and at best too
slow. If the Consul seems slack, cable to
Pauline and Mary to set machinery in motion in
Hongkong for a direct appeal to the Foreign
Office. I dined with the Governor once in
Hongkong, and though his aide-de-camp seemed*

*to ignore common rules of precedence in placing
me, I suppose he could hardly refuse to use his
influence in effecting my release. I tell you I am
damned uncomfortable.*

" The messenger is just loading up," said
Rodd. " Anything to send Heming? "

Ipsie sent him a note:

" *I wish my thoughts would make things
easier for you, my dear; if they could, you'd wear
an armour of my thoughts and lie on a feather
bed of blessings.*"

When she had finished writing she thought,
" I am a hypocrite. Also, to be even a little
fanciful to Jacob is waste of fancies." Yet
she imagined with horror his discomfort and
loneliness. She was a coldly tender-hearted
person, not a loving one.

She found more and more irritating
Pauline's rather unconvinced and uncon-
vincing assumptions as to her feelings. At
dinner on this first night at Yueh Lai Chou
she could have been gay in spite of her weariness. She could always be gay if she found
herself charming, and with Rodd's gay

attentive face opposite to her she felt herself surely a potential success. But Pauline would allow no one but the absent Jacob to be a success. Jacob must be the melancholy life and soul of the party. Mrs. Hinds, sodden with sorrow and with a severe cold in the head, spoke only through her handkerchief. Pauline stroked her Sophie's hand whenever it was available. She would have stroked Ipsie's hand if it had been nearer, but the pressure would have been gently disapproving.

"We are oddly thrown together, we four," said Pauline. "Held together by a common suspense. It's hard on you, Mr. Innes, having to look after three tense-hearted women whose thoughts are away in the mountains. But we're going to be as brave and as cheerful as we can, aren't we, little sister, aren't we, dearest Sophie. Courage has to be such a big part of the lives of women."

Ipsie, in spite of her irritation, found her face mechanically assuming the wistful expression of one whose beloved is in danger.

" Oh, don't let's be too brave," said Rodd, smiling rather fixedly at Pauline. " Let's just be natural."

He thought, " Why, they're devouring Ipsie between them. Some day there'll be nothing left of her."

CHAPTER IX

Ipsie was ill. The cough and the weariness
that had followed her up from Hongkong
had reached a small but startling climax in a
spot of blood upon her handkerchief. Dr.
Marrowby seemed to think very little of it.

"Just a touch," he said happily, as though
he had arranged the thing himself as a
pleasant surprise for Ipsie. "Taken right
at the beginning like this . . . pure mountain air. Most of us have harboured the
germ without knowing it at some time or
another in our lives. Just a matter of
resistance in getting rid of the little beggar.
Very good thing he made himself known so
early."

Ipsie stayed in bed for two or three days.
It was the first time she had ever been ill.

PIPERS AND A DANCER

Bed seemed a sordid thing; one only felt
·calm and clean for half an hour after the bed
was made, and after that one was lost and
entangled in a jungle of books, old letters,
newspapers, brushes and combs, cold hot-
water bottles and sheets that had come un-
tucked. Ipsie wondered if courtesans who
slept in silks and the scent of fresh violets
had similar difficulties. In spite of the
physical discomfort of the moment the future
seemed romantic to her. She was reprieved
from marriage and yet was a centre of
interest. She could be loved now, she
hoped, but she need not love. She need
not at any rate decide about love. She
posed herself conventionally milk-pale and
spiritual with the conventional hectic flush
on each hollow cheek. All the voices of her
imagination were hushed and almost reverent.

" Such nonsense," she thought, and drew
a mocking drawing of a lily-like simpering
nude with an angular droop, very small and
neglected against a tempestuous large background of passers -. by. " I draw, I think,

to give myself a loophole so that when I am dead and remember what a fool I was, I can think of what I drew and say—'Yes, I was a fool, but by God, I almost knew it.'"

"I suppose I mustn't marry now," she said to Dr. Marrowby, and her Showman made her say it in a brave but broken voice.

But doctors are apparently used to showmen. "You'll have to get rid of your trouble first, of course. And for that you don't need doctors or medicines so much as good air, good food and your own native good sense."

Ipsie felt guilty. "My good sense isn't native," she thought. "What there is of it is just a naturalised alien."

Pauline was extremely kind to Ipsie. Ipsie now seemed to be at Pauline's mercy. A small horizontal beneficiary cannot maintain spiritual independence in the presence of a large vertical benefactress. The room seemed generously full of Pauline nearly always. When Pauline went away Ipsie could not help feeling like a blind puppy whose warm, enormous and indispensable mother has left it for a while. But Pauline did not leave her much. Pauline knew the whole condescending and suffocating art of devotion. There was no limit to her kindness; she even ministered to Ipsie's poses. Ipsie was irresistibly obliged to be a patient, brave little thing in the presence of Pauline. And something barely conscious in the depths of Pauline's nature said, *I have her now*.

In a few days Ipsie was allowed to transplant her business of resting on to the verandah. The air was merry and warm and the mountains looked over the white wall of the garden. The butterflies planed and twinkled round a big bush of heliotrope. Little violet dice fell on the verandah from the wan eucalyptus trees that overhung the garden.

Ipsie secretly called Mrs. Hinds " an attemptuous person." Sophie was full of helpful ideas that never inspired spontaneous enthusiasm. She was obsessed by the loving fear that Ipsie, left to herself, would " brood." She therefore often shewed Ipsie photographs

of women friends with glasses and flat hair—
"Oh, such a lovely soul!"—and snapshots of
groups that did not include herself, thus
denying Ipsie even the meagre excitement of
saying, " Oh yes, I see you now, there in the
back row, but, my *dear*, it's *dreadful* of you."
Sophie read to Ipsie from the American
magazines which were the vessel into which
she poured her soul. Sophie Hinds was a
prophetess not without honour in her own
country, and her messages were always con-
spicuously printed, although they were, like
all other messages similarly conveyed, out-
shouted by clamorous challenges from the
margins—*Have You a Skin You'd Love to
Touch?—Are You at Ease in High Society?—
Can You Hold His Love?—Motor to Church
in Comfort.* Thin tepid columns of Sophie's
message ran down the strident pages like
tears down the face of a shrieking woman.
Sophie read various messages aloud to Ipsie,
but she would not read her own. She would,
on reaching the headlines of one of her own
contributions, crush the pages into Ipsie's

hands saying, " I can't read this right out loud, it means too much to me. But you read it to yourself, lady dear, and don't hesitate to be completely frank about your reaction to it." Pauline would laugh affectionately and say, " Sophie's a mass of temperament."

Pauline was Sophie's perfect listener, and could be so implicitly relied on to say the right thing that Sophie actually consented to bring forth a neat, coy, unpublished notebook full of formless Thoughts. These Thoughts cried aloud for a constructive hearer, and this Pauline energetically proved herself to be. Sophie was often obliged to conceal her surprise at her own profundity. " Sophie, Sophie, you have a genius for leaving exactly the right amount unsaid," applauded Pauline, and Mrs. Hinds, who had intended in each thought to say everything, was naturally much delighted to find that she had, so to speak, failed so successfully. She decided to publish the book of Thoughts for the benefit of a public of Paulines.

PIPERS AND A DANCER

Curiously enough there was another and absurdly different path into Mrs. Hinds' good graces, and this path Rodd had discovered. Rodd had an instinct for pleasing people who mattered little to him, and his successful method of approach to Sophie was a cautious impertinence. He addressed her in a loud restraining manner as though she were a wild woman; expressed fears for Donnie Marrowby's moral safety within reach of Sophie's wiles; called her Madcap Sophie . . . Sunbeam Sophie. . . . He continued these rather fatiguing tactics until he was disgusted with himself, but he could not resist a means to popularity, and it was obvious that Mrs. Hinds was never tired of this method. She was very much delighted with his simple liberties. Rodd, she assured every one, was nothing but a great big tease, she slapped him ecstatically on the arm, and wrote a Message on the Duty of Joy in Bereavement. But there was a check when Rodd, haranguing her under the improvised name of Sophonisba Mildred, was struck dumb on seeing tears gleaming behind Sophie's pince-nez. "Oh, never mind . . . I know you didn't mean it. . . . Such a queer coincidence. . . . Mildred, my little sister who died. . . ."

"Just like Sophie to have a little dead sister Mildred at such an inconvenient moment," said Rodd to Ipsie when Pauline's ready arm had enveloped and led away the sniffing Sophie. "I feel as if I daren't ever smile again."

Pauline did not approve of Rodd's jocular treatment of Sophie. A protégé of Pauline's should be reverently treated. But Pauline, mercifully, shrank out of doors. She could not dominate or fill the blue-and-brown sunlit garden as she had filled the sick-room. She was, however, as benevolent as ever; she would not willingly relinquish her advantage. Ipsie, she felt, might still be gathered to her bosom, and Jacob, even if he married her, might thus be kept in the family. Pauline was a spacious entertainer; she told many anecdotes, often about Jacob. Ipsie

was left, however, with the impression that
the Heming family was unfortunate in being
uniquely devoid of real family jokes. Family
jokes, of course, though rightly cursed by
strangers, are the bond that keeps most
families alive.

Rodd's welcome expression of sympathy
in Ipsie's illness was the gift of a piebald
mongrel puppy which he and Ipsie called
Tiffany because its price—if any—was above
rubies. This explanation always inspired
Donnie Marrowby to sing, "fatter than
butter—yea, than much fine butter" to
Purcell in F minor. Tiffany was a jocose but
rather cold-hearted puppy who walked as
though he had never worn stays. He barked
with his mouth full, and indeed had no
manners at all. "An ideal size, a puppy
—a fairy size," said Ipsie. "I'd like to
have a little man just that size. Sensible
hedonistic puppies like women best because
women have webbed laps."

Ipsie had become a little more prosaic in
the eyes of Rodd since she had come to

PIPERS AND A DANCER

Yueh Lai Chou. He several times congratulated himself on the fact that her attraction for him was not very strong. But he was still acutely averse to the idea of her becoming a Heming. He had taken an immediate dislike to Pauline. Jacob, though tiresome, had accidentally given Rodd an outlet for his tenderness of heart. Pauline gave Rodd nothing, not even—for the first week—an excuse to detest her. Rodd was a very lazy young man; he not only never troubled to impose impressions on others, but he would not accept from others deliberately imposed impressions. Pauline, being entirely alien, did not interest him. He took no cynical academic pleasure in the alien personality at all. No person was a study to him. He was too lazy to take a place in any audience; he insisted always on a small but smiling part among the supers on the stage. Compassion was the only emotion that ever inspired him to inquire personally into the motives of others. He intensely valued easiness; he laughed easily and pitied easily.

PIPERS AND A DANCER

He asked little of people — only that they should not insist too much on their own personalities and that they should not too much probe or despise his. Most people, therefore, were sympathetic to him. But he never found stale the recurring delight of being able to say, after two or three words with a stranger, " *Yes*, this is my kind of person."

Pauline did not approve of the presentation of Tiffany the puppy.

" Dear Mr. Innes, how like a man! . . ." she said, looming over Ipsie and Rodd with a cherishing smile. *How like a man* was a very well-defined reproach on Pauline's lips, just as *How like a woman* always prefaced some sounding enthusiasm about sacrifice. " So this stuffy little creature is to sit always on our childie's lap breathing up the pure air that the mountains are wafting her? "

Pauline was an artist in getting her own way. When she saw that Ipsie no longer wore her " little childie " expression she began at once, with elaborate playfulness, to fondle Tiffany. " Well, well, Tiffany, if

you have fleas, forbear to shed them now."
She was always especially kind to people
who wanted their own way. Even when
they got their own way Pauline seldom
sulked. She had too earnest a conscience.
It is permissible, however, to be aloofly
pensive in such circumstances. But in
this case Pauline expected victory, so she
was agreeable, told an anecdote of a little
boy saying his prayers, talked about the
marvels of space—even, presently, sub-
mitted the time-worn story of Jacob and
Maidie at Panama.

" A little wisp of a dear waif, Maidie was,
Jacob has often told me—and these great
rough men round her, sneering, bullying.
. . . He said she looked like a hunted thing
—until she met his eyes, and then her face
was lit up with hope. She went up to him
quite simply and put her hand in his like a
little child. You, loving our Jacob, little
sister, know what it was she found in his
eyes. He took her home as he would have
taken a strayed baby. . . ."

PIPERS AND A DANCER

Pauline liked very much talking of little pathetic people.

" The protection of the weak is almost a weakness with my brother, Mr. Innes," she continued. " Our Jacob, for all his apparent practical and prosaic good sense, is always seeking . . . seeking. . . ."

" I don't doubt it," agreed Rodd placidly. " I've often heard him describe that scene in Panama—though you've abridged it considerably, Miss Heming, and somehow given it a literary twist."

" Seeking . . . seeking . . ." continued Pauline inexorably. " Always on the trail of something half-known—that is Jacob's history in a nutshell. Till our little Ipsie shone like a star across his path and ended his seeking."

" Stars have paths too," said Rodd. " But most stars stick to them."

" Jacob is fortunate in anchoring his star," said Pauline with a touch of doubt in her fine serious voice.

" Indeed yes, he is fortunate," said Rodd

with a polite lack of emphasis. It made him a little happy to talk of Ipsie as a star.

Pauline tenderly stroked Ipsie's hair as she rose with the intention of thwarting Ipsie's hopes by finding a strap, chain and soap-box for Tiffany the puppy.

" Don't tire my childie, talking," she said as she went away along the verandah.

" I don't believe," said Rodd, " that you and Miss Heming are at your best together."

" I'm not at my best with any one," said Ipsie, delighted. " I have no Best. Or rather my Best changes with my company. I adopt other people's Bests and *be* them. I shall be at your Best now till half-past five, and then I must go in."

" Don't," said Rodd. " You'll lose yourself that way."

" I lost myself long ago. When I was born, I think."

Rodd meditated. He found that he quite tenderly regretted the fact that Ipsie had been lost at birth. " Well, if you must be lost, don't lose yourself in Pauline Heming or in Sophie Hinds, or in people who have died, or in——" His gentlemanly tongue shied at the difficult name of Heming. " You can go out into the wilderness, but you needn't have a second-rate taste in wildernesses. I guess it's just that some wildernesses are flowery and some aren't."

" How extraordinary," said Ipsie after a pause, " to hear any one being eloquent about any one else! I never could—only about myself."

" What self is that ? " asked Rodd. " I thought your self was lost."

" Perhaps not lost so much as unknown. Perhaps not unknown so much as too well known. Or perhaps I have a self that can't shut the door; my self goes out every minute and other people's selves come in."

" You're not being my Best now," said Rodd.

" Yes, I am trying to be. But I haven't travelled in many wildernesses with so few landmarks and trails as yours. You see, with Pauline and with Jacob and with Victor

158

and with Mother, there's no doubt about which of me they want. With you—I don't know."

"Oh, Ipsie, Ipsie . . ." said Rodd, and he looked away from her suddenly to the slate-black clouds that were given a fantastic emphasis behind the pale stagey trees by the sharp light. Rodd found his mind instantly as clear as the low light that filled the valley. He knew now that he was being forced to know her too well. He had insisted all his life on choosing an easy path among smiling easy men and women of his own stature— and now here was a giant in his path. The subtle signal—*This is certainly my kind of person*—generally inspired by a gay and commonplace remark, had meant, *This is a person to whom I can talk without effort and to whom I can listen without embarrassment.* But now of Ipsie he had clear knowledge, *This is a person whom I must think of for the rest of my life and perhaps never know. Effort or no effort, disaster or no disaster, this is a person who interrupts ease for ever.*

PIPERS AND A DANCER

Ipsie watched his face eagerly and hoped that her hair, which she felt to be untidy, was nevertheless looking light and curly.. She hoped that he was thinking her pretty though he would not look at her.   And under these little glowing hopes she despised herself bitterly   " Every one has nobility and escape but me."

CHAPTER X

Ipsie often imagined people so vividly that she thought she might perhaps claim to enjoy psychic experiences. She had been thinking of Rodd as she lay in the sun rubbing the twitching ear of the puppy Tiffany. She had been wondering innocently if she might call herself in love with him, and if so why love must be for her this vain and painless matter. For real women love was the tree on which the fruit of life was hung; for Ipsie love was a spray of peach-blossom in a fine wind. It had no root in her. Nothing that she knew, nothing that she desired seemed really rooted in her. Love for her was compounded of small blossoming pleasures, the pleasure of gratified vanity, the desire for experience, the deter-

M

mination to miss nothing that others possessed, the excitement of untried mental
intimacy, intoxicating insecurity, the pleasure
her eyes took in faces, a thrilling pain in the
diaphragm in the presence of a man—these
were her pleasures in love. There was, she
realised, something missing—*given* love was
missing. Whenever she realised this she
felt cruelly defrauded and loathed herself.
If she had been conscious of failure in the
eyes of Rodd—as she had been conscious
before when crossing the Pacific with him—
her vanity would have been a little hurt and
she would have held herself deliberately in-
different to him. But she watched herself
with outside eyes, she appraised herself with
outside eyes, and now, being almost certain
that Rodd valued her, she valued herself and,
through herself, vaguely but delightfully
valued him.

After thinking about Rodd and about
love she thought of Conrad. Conrad was
all life in her thoughts; he was never irrele-
vant; sometimes she thought that she could

hardly consider herself virgin, she lived so
intensely in Conrad. She had lived in
him much more intensely since he died.
Sometimes it seemed to her that she had not
very much loved the actual Conrad, the thin,
pale-haired, sleepy Conrad who used to dress
in a dark grey suit, sometimes suffered from
ear-ache and was forever sucking at his pipe
with discreet bubbling noises and then light-
ing it again clumsily while vital discussions
hung waiting on the air. The Conrad who
never could be at his best at the right time,
failed in exams, missed balls at tennis at the
moment when all eyes were upon him,
uttered social blunders in unexpected silences,
the Conrad whom silly women loved in spite
of all discouragement. Ipsie could never
have said whether she loved him very intensely or not, but she knew the patterns of
his ties as well as she knew her own hats;
his best-loved possessions—his Malay kris,
his little green glass horse blown under the
eye of an aunt in Venice, his first edition of
The Master of Ballantrae—had, long before

he died, been as holy and as radiant in her eyes as in his. His first love affair and his first pawnbroker's ticket had been to her, as to him, real and almost terrifying initiations into grown-upness. Through Conrad she not only learned of prostitutes and polo, of the different merits of shaving soap and of indecent chanteys—but these things entered into her personal experience, they became important and commonplace to her like the intimate facts of her own life and her own body. She had not consciously loved Conrad, alive, so much as known him. Yet behind that living, contentious, charming, unfortunate Conrad there was some one imprisoned, something imprisoned, perfection imprisoned. When Conrad died, the door of the prison opened and the prisoner perfection was free to walk the world with Ipsie, to give the visions of her eyes their colour, to give her all the ecstasy she was ever to know. . . . The freed prisoner perfection, who wore Conrad's face, sprang to her eyes whenever she made picturable statements to herself. . . .

PIPERS AND A DANCER

*He was there waiting. . . . Human beauty.
. . . God. . . . Up guards and at 'em. . . .
Coming home with good news. . . . Could you
ever love me. . . .* Words were instinct with
him, and every line she saw; but not the lines
she drew, for she put her vanity, her sense of
humour, her cynicism and herself into her
drawing, not perfection.

She lay in the sun, having passed from a
practical meditation about Rodd to a strange
dream of Conrad—and suddenly she thought
of Jacob Heming. She was sure that she
saw him as he was. She saw him sitting on
red soil with his back against an abrupt low
cliff. He had her letter in his hand and he
was looking intently and sadly at the toe
of his boot, thinking of wee Mary. The
brigands, in dark stiff-quilted coats, crouching in the thick undergrowth of the mountain
side below the level of Jacob's sandstone
throne, were smoking and talking in under-
tones and looking, furtively and often, at
Jacob.

" I'm sure that is a true dream," thought

Ipsie as she collected the vivid details of it behind her eyes. " I shall ask him when I see him, but even without asking him I know it's true."

It was not true.

Jacob Heming was sitting on the wet grass that had sprung in a ruined mud hut; the surviving corner of the roof was partly sheltering him from a prolonged storm of rain. The mountains were blotted out and the low wet trees swung desolately in a cold whining wind. Some of Heming's captors sat at a distance of a few feet from him. He could smell them all the time. They were all arguing furiously about small sums of money; coppers rattled in vehemently demonstrating palms. One of them wore a harsh blue woollen cape made primitively of an unsewn square of material slung about the shoulders by a straw cord. This was the small shrivelled man who did Heming's cooking. This man was emaciated; it seemed that his lips were the only fleshy part of him; when he spoke his lips writhed

upward and backward so that the inner side
of the lips could be seen; his brown legs
were incredibly thin so that the big feet
looked deformed. The other men shivered
under the common Yunnan coolie rain-
shield, made of some thick blackish fibre
that had the half-bald unkempt look of a
buffalo's hide, and stiff as a tortoise's shell.
One of these men was a big fellow with very
stiff cropped hair; his whole face seemed
smoothly ample except his nose, which was
nearly flat, and his small eyes, which were like
the dark stone of a fruit seen through the
clean-slit skin. The third man had a manner
which exasperated Jacob even more than did
all the other exasperating details of his experience. The man's manner was obsequi-
ous and always watchful. He could speak
a few words of French and said that he had
been a French priest's boy and that he was a
Christian. He called his associates " pas-
moyen-bon " and laughed wheezily as he
did so. He wore good green jade and silver
bangles on his wrists and a roll of good silk

inside his turban. All three wore wide hats on which the rain tapped and bounced. The hats, made of saffron-coloured straw, were like shallow pyramids with round bases; they were perched either on the big untidy blue turbans or else on stiff red cotton circlets which balanced precariously on the men's cropped or shaven skulls. From within the hats dangled long tassels in magenta or green.

Jacob, at ease or not at ease, never noticed details. He knew the faces of his personal guard only when he looked at them. He had no visual memory. All Chinese had, for him, the same hated face. He hated without observing it.

Jacob had scarcely ever in his life been happy, though he gave each new grievance the credit of novelty. There were no degrees in his resentments—a thoughtless remark that seemed to him ill-timed, the interruption of one of his lamentable songs, the loss of his mother or of a ten dollar note had given him almost the same sick shocking feeling of anger as did his present distresses in captivity. The small discomforts of being a prisoner affected him as much as did the large. He had always been sartorially unlucky; he had always suffered—in spite of the most serious precautions—from the devilishness of clothes. A conspiracy of tailors and outfitters, as it seemed to him, caused him always to be nipped at the arm-pits by waistcoats, irked across the back by coats, deserted by studs, tortured by shoes, blistered by socks, betrayed by sock-sus-penders and braces. . . . He was a man ridden always by ridiculous and desperate goblins. Thus he was now the prisoner, not only of the brigands but of his clothes. His riding-breeches, wet and stale with rain and incessant wear, clipped him so tightly under the knees that his legs swelled; his high boots, which had always seemed to him rather smart and gratifying, now gave him agony; his fastidiousness revolted against the dirty shirt that, for warmth, he must continue to wear.

PIPERS AND A DANCER

He was obsessed by the dirt of his surroundings. In his mouth continually he seemed to taste dirt. He moved his tongue about his mouth and thought that he tasted death after every dreadful meal. The rice that he had to eat so constantly was grey and flecked with black; he hated and feared it so much that the expectation of a meal would sometimes make him violently sick. He was hysterically conscious of his stomach now as a nucleus of death. He built no hopes on the arrival of the provisions from Yueh Lai Chou, for he had convinced himself that by now his body was built on a foundation of death. No help that could come now could take the thick dangerous taste of fever and dirt from his palate.

He was indeed very feverish, but, curiously enough, he did not realise it. The pain in his joints and the nervous loathing of the food that he had eaten and must eat again seemed to take a kind of shape in his mind as pillars of a monstrous dark doorway through which strange visitors came in to

bewilder him. Often one half of his con-
sciousness was comforted by a hope that the
other half knew to be false. He would see
a signal of secret encouragement, a meaning
glance of sympathy in the hard hated eyes of
one of his guard, and think perhaps this was
the kind of British spy one reads about,
whose disguise is perfect and method unfailing. He would see a hint of soldiers
coming stealthily among the low distant
shrubs of azalea. He would see a fluttering
paper half hidden in a hand or hear a creaking step behind the wall of his hut. And as
he imagined these things he would breathe a
sweet air of comfort, only to find it turning
sour on his palate as he realised abruptly the
fearful emptiness of his world. Once he distinctly heard a whisper—*Heming, Heming*—
and though he knew that he deceived himself, he buttressed the deceit with a structure
of desperate artificial conviction. A whisper
like that could only mean help and safety in
this company of brawling harsh voices; no
enemy would whisper to him; there was

some one compassionate near him. The whisper ran like pure cool wine through the hot channels of his brain. And even after he had realised that the sound was made by the wet leaves of a weed moving against a wall in the wind, there remained an aroma of hope in his empty heart like the aroma of good wine in a cup just drained.

Across the threshold of the gargoyled doorway of his confusion came strangers and friends. Himself again and again, sometimes as a stranger and sometimes as a friend. Himself as he remembered himself in the bar of a hotel in Panama, irritably emptying a drowned highball on to the dusty floor before the sheepishly smiling bartender; himself absurdly complaining of the heat on the Bund in Shanghai—the merciful crisp heat of the sun that was hidden from him now; himself dining at Government House in Hongkong and noticing that his nails were dirty and beating the aide-de-camp at billiards; himself looking sulkily at Winchester Cathedral with Ipsie Mary and her aunt with whom they were staying—(Ipsie Mary chattered of a picture she would draw and call *Different People Looking at Jane Austen's Tomb*, a simpleton's title, Jacob had thought—pictures should be called *Autumn Leaves* or *Her First Kiss* or *His Majesty the Baby* or by other reputable names); himself teaching Maidie to sing ' Sweet Marie.' . . .

Maidie had been the one triumphant success of his life, and ever since she had left him he had despised pure women, though he did not know this. Only in the person of Maidie had life proved itself adaptable to Jacob Heming. Maidie had loved his singing; Maidie had admitted many times that people almost always behaved detestably to him in spite of his goodness; Maidie had not cost him much either—she was a saving little puss. Her mother, Jacob thought, had lured her away from him. Like all ideal women, Maidie was adaptable and easily influenced. Her mother, a snakey old Mexican, had certainly told her lies about the impeccable Jacob. For surely, surely,

PIPERS AND A DANCER

Maidie had loved him. . . . . *Sweet Marie,*
come to me, Come to me, Sweet Marie. . . .
Songs were always loud and sweet in his ears
though they wheezed absurdly through his
lips. The song ran like a seeking bird
through the empty room that he remembered,
seeking the laughing small Maidie who was
gone. Fever tore the scales from Jacob's
dull eyes; he could see himself standing
aghast in the doorway of that empty room,
himself, the great shrinking shell of a broken
heart. He could see the sunny room quite
distinctly and the moving-picture magazine
that Maidie had been reading. And how
repellent it was that Ipsie Mary, not Maidie,
should be standing by that big holy bed,
chattering . . . chattering like a little boy
about feelings and fancies. Well, Ipsie Mary
was inevitable now and he would cure her of
fancies. She should learn to minister to a
man; she should learn to be a woman and to
sew and to listen. Women worthy of the
name do not scribble in drawing-books
while men talk—they sew. The roundness

of Ipsie Mary's face fascinated Jacob as he thought of it; it deceived him into imagining that she would quickly attain to a plump docile middle age. He thought coldly but hungrily of Ipsie Mary; he could not visualise her face at all, but he thought of her in a clean trim blue frock, clean and a little bleak, like Sunday in London. He associated Sunday in London with Ipsie Mary; in his dark quivering doorway was framed a picture of Ipsie Mary waiting for him at a bus-stop, tapping her foot on the pavement and looking about quickly and keenly. Looking for him, tapping her foot because she was impatient for him. She was always the first at a rendezvous. Jacob himself was always deliberately last; he felt that lateness upheld his dignity. Of course he had never been able to practise this theory on Maidie. To Maidie two hours, three hours, a whole afternoon, a cinema ticket bought in vain—were nothing. And to Jacob now as he dimly saw the figure of Maidie coming towards him, jerking her hips, looking into passing men's faces—it seemed that years of waiting for her were not in vain. Maidie created largeness and patience in men, it seemed. He remembered the anecdote that he had so often told to people who never seemed sufficiently interested. The anecdote was quite unlike the real story, but he retold it to an ideal listening silence now. Maidie had been so tiny, and her bruised arms and breast so small when she showed them. She picked Jacob out of all the men present. The point of the anecdote was the largeness of Jacob, the smallness of Maidie. The end of the anecdote was, " I said to all those big hulking brutes who were sneering at her—' If any one wants to stand up to me right here and now just let him say so and I'm his man—but if any one says another word to the young lady —I'll paint the floor red with the lot of you! ' And then every one heard the rattling of teeth and what d'you think it was? Why the bartender—terrified out of his life—hiding under the bar. . . ." Ha-ha-ha-ha. . . .

PIPERS AND A DANCER

What had he really said ?   He had forgotten
now.   The anecdote of Jacob and Maidie
ended there—the story of Jacob and Maidie
began.   Ipsie Mary was small too, small
and bleak like a boy.   Going out with Ipsie
Mary on Sundays was like going out with a
queer boy, the kind of boy you can't take
into a bar.   She would learn to be a woman
but she would never learn to be Maidie.
Ipsie Mary had fancies—Maidie had only
one fancy, a fancy man.   Ipsie Mary had
fancies that seemed deliberately queer.   She
would not go with him to the country on
Sundays; she would not join a crowd.   They
rode on the tops of buses to the City; there
was no one in the City on Sundays, no fun at
all.   However, in the little streets about St.
Paul's and Cheapside there was silence and
opportunity for Ipsie Mary to learn to listen
to Jacob.   She could often listen quite
nicely for nearly a whole afternoon; she
would only begin to chatter, perhaps, at
about six, when they were nearly home, so it
didn't matter much.   There was something

177   N

about her white odd face that apologised for
her chatter. She would end by understanding what a man wanted of a woman, of that
he felt sure. Marriage taught even fanciful
women that.

His heart seemed to drop suddenly as he
remembered where he was. The rain poured
from the fragment of roof in stripes before
his eyes. His feet were like fish, so cold,
moving without being felt. He felt terribly
ill. Some catastrophe was upon him. A
burning, shivering spasm shook him ridicu-
lously about. There were no friends, there
was no help. Maidie . . . Maidie. . . .

Even the mountains were rolling and
swinging.

CHAPTER XI

MR. MORDAUNT, the British Consul from Yunnan-fu, had come to Yueh Lai Chou to see about Jacob's release.

" You can see," said Pauline to Rodd, " that this affair has been a great blow to him. He is evidently a great friend of our dear Jacob's. One of the comforts of adversity is that it brings out the friendship men feel for each other."

The Consul, a very tall awkward man with greying red hair like fire smothered in ashes, expressed no affection for Jacob. Being a sentimentalist he had been interested in Ipsie's existence on hearing of it before he met her. But, as he was a sentimentalist, he felt on meeting her that she had somehow missed her cue. So she had. Though, as a rule, very attentive to the rôle she imagined was expected of her, she did this time miss her cue. She was not accustomed to sentimentalists, and thought, when Mr. Mordaunt called her a " plucky little woman," that he said it in approval. She was therefore plucky to excess, smiled, thrust her chin out, did not implore the Consul to save her Jacob, did not even allow her lips to tremble. The Consul thought that modern girls were heartless creatures.

Mordaunt, like most sentimental men, believed that the endangering of a chance of marriage was the most appalling disaster that could overtake a woman. Even though he considered Heming a bounder he thought that any girl should be glad to marry him.

Ipsie liked Mr. Mordaunt very much. She liked his gravity, his gentle voice and his manner of listening attentively to whatever she said. She thought that he liked her and was very glad that she had come to China, where she was conscious, for the first time in her life, of intermittent personal success.

PIPERS AND A DANCER

She was feeling comparatively strong again now, was happy in the attention of Rodd, and was attracted also by young Donnie Marrowby, an ugly serene boy of seventeen who was often sent over by his mother to play the guitar and sing to Ipsie —a mission which he interpreted literally; he never spoke to Ipsie but only sang.

Ipsie thought often of Jacob in the same spirit as one, feeling herself drifting from the Faith, might often say a prayer with an effort and so snatch at a precarious self-respect.

The Consul had told her that a Chinese colonel, the emissary of the Governor-General of Yunnan, had passed through Yueh Lai Chou with an escort of soldiers to open negotiations with the brigands.

Ipsie shut her mind against the thought of Jacob's return. She never had an acute sense of the future and, when she was in doubt, she could, at will, refuse to-morrow admission to her imagination. She was aware that humiliation and difficulty lay before her, but it did not seem to matter very much until it reached her. During the War she and Conrad used to be genuinely and wildly happy up to the last moment of his leave—even during the wait on Victoria Station. She had the power of entrenching herself safely in a short happy minute. She therefore lived peacefully and gaily during the days that followed the Chinese colonel's departure. She did not realise that the atmosphere about her was one of suspense until one afternoon when Pauline, who had been out for a walk under God's sky, rushed home with her dress blowing like a banner, calling, " Great news, great news. . . ."

Mrs. Hinds gave a discordant creaking cry, " Oh, at last . . ." and, though Mrs. Hinds had never been taciturn, the effect of that cry was that of the breaking of a long unbearable silence. Only then did Ipsie—chancily tender-hearted—know that the feeling about her had been intense. " Why, they really love him," she thought, and she began to cry. Her own pretending made her feel outcast.

PIPERS AND A DANCER

Pauline put her arm round Ipsie's shoulders. " This is better, this is better," thought Pauline. Superiority brought out the best in her. She felt a genuine impulse of affection for Ipsie.

" I was too sudden, dearest. Naughty bearish old Pauline has startled the little pale babe in the wood. But they say good news never harms. Listen, you two brave darlings; Jacob will come soon now. Colonel Hsu let the Consul know that the matter was being arranged with quite unexpected success; the brigands seemed quite half-hearted in trying to make terms. Perhaps they are frightened by the stir their important capture has made in China; perhaps darling Jacob is rather too lion-like a prisoner; perhaps they have some new plan which a prisoner obstructs. At any rate Colonel Hsu made very few concessions indeed, and though the brigands blustered at first they gave in at last and will send our dear one back to us within the week."

Her fluency seemed maddening to Ipsie,

183

who was trembling with the sense of half-understood and portentous events.

Pauline went on, looking strangely at Ipsie's fixed and frightened face. " So now my little sister must smile through her tears. Only a few to-morrows to wait—a few to-morrows more or less will seem nothing when they have all turned into yesterdays. You who are so full of pretty fancies, dearest, fancy now that you see Jacob coming—as he will come one of these to-morrows—round the clump of bamboos at the gate."

Ipsie obediently fancied. She was horrified to see the fancied Jacob frowning and heavy against the light well-kempt reeds of the distant lake. Jacob's face would loom over the heliotrope. The disturbance of his coming would disperse the butterflies.

Ipsie knew now that she had hoped never to see him again.

People should dissolve like clouds, like the thin shell-white clouds that cross the quiet faces of the mountains and, pleasantly and without pain, cease to exist. It was intolerable that words must be spoken, long sustained poses destroyed, anger created, self-regard torn in shreds, before two people could dissolve from before each other's faces.

Ipsie's Showman held her helpless. It was a one-man showman's strike. The Showman definitely refused to exhibit to Ipsie and the world the shocking tableau of Ipsie's imagination. A stuttering, sobbing Ipsie. . . . " No, no, Jacob . . . it isn't that. . . . I'm not frivolous . . . I'm not faithless . . . I just don't love any one at all . . . I never shall . . . you came nearest. . . . Oh, Jacob, let me out . . . don't hate me. . . . Don't make me hate myself. . . ." Jacob would never let her out. Jacob was secure in his confidence in wee Mary—who had never existed. Pauline had Ipsie prisoner in chains of brass. Mrs. Hinds added, in Ipsie's imagination, an alarming cubit to her stature. Donnie would bring a schoolboy's sense of honour to bear, Rodd, a grown man's — both as imagined by women. Dr. Marrowby,

PIPERS AND A DANCER

Captain Norman, Mr. Mordaunt, would turn away their kind appreciative faces.

The Showman refused to give such a show. The Showman had turned censor.

" Why did I get well? Why didn't Jacob die? "

After a moment she thought coldly, " And besides, Jacob paid my passage out."

" Here comes Donnie," said Pauline radiantly. " Donnie, sing us a joyful song. We are joyful. We have good news of our dear man."

Donnie replied with a few harsh chords. Guitars, pianos, Chinese flutes, were part of Donnie—extensions, as it were, to his natural body. Notes were breathed by Donnie as quiet air is breathed by other people. He would talk to the tune of his guitar and think to the murmured accompaniment of the piano. Persons who replied to him found themselves taking part in a soft recitative which was so natural that it did not seem irksome. It never occurred to Donnie that music should be confined to ruled books

coyly produced at the repeated invitation of
hostesses, that a performance should be pre-
luded by, " I'm afraid I'm awfully out of
practice," and followed by, " Yes, that's a
favourite little thing of mine," and a retire-
ment into renewed coyness. He was a
pensive, self-confident boy. While Ipsie was
ill Donnie's guitar sprawled on Heming's
drawing-room sofa. Pauline sat down on
it sometimes by mistake, striking an unexpected chord.

She pluckéd off her high-heeled shoes
A-made of Spanish leather-O,
She would in the street with her bare, bare feet,
Along with the wraggle-taggle gypsies-O.

O, saddle to me my milk-white steed
And saddle to me my pony-O,
That I may ride and seek my bride
Who is gone with the wraggle-taggle gypsies-O.

To Ipsie, Donnie's young pale tenor voice
was exactly the voice of her dreams. Perfection was come.

There was some one coming round the
clump of bamboos at the gate. Ipsie held

her breath. It was Rodd. He stood beside the heliotrope bush, listening to the song. The butterflies were not disturbed.

What makes you leave your house and land?
Your golden treasure for to go?
What makes you leave your new-wedded lord
To run with the wraggle-taggle gypsies-O?

Ah, what care I for my house and land?
What care I for my money-O?
And what care I for my new-wedded lord,
For I'm off with the wraggle-taggle gypsies-O.

Last night you slept in a goosefeather bed
With the sheet turned down so bravely-O,
But to-night you'll sleep in a cold open field
Along with the wraggle-taggle gypsies-O.

Ah, what care I for your goosefeather bed
With the sheet turned down so bravely-O,
For to-night I'll sleep in a cold open field
Along with the wraggle-taggle gypsies-O.

" That song," said Rodd, " reminds me a little of you, Ipsie."

There was Ipsie, safely posed again, wild, brave Ipsie, what cared she for a goose-feather bed, she was off with the wraggle-taggle gypsies-O. Followed, of course, by the charmed eyes of Rodd. Jacob was left looking silly beside the kicked-off shoes in the turret-room.

"Gypsy-Ipsie," said Pauline inevitably. "Well, Gypsy-Ipsie must wraggle-taggle indoors. That shawl isn't thick enough. And listen, children, I have an idea. We'll have Mr. Mordaunt and the Marrowbys to dinner and open a bottle of Jacob's champagne to Jacob's quick return."

"All right, let him come," thought Ipsie, and she wished she dared kiss Rodd and kiss Donnie and dance round the heliotrope with the butterflies.

It was a warm still night crowned with a full moon. Dinner was out of doors under dark grape-red lanterns strung to the bleached sinuous bough of a eucalyptus tree.

Mr. Mordaunt tried to interest Mrs. Hinds in Yunnanese politics. He was excited by the description *journalist*. To be talking to some one who was paid to write for a newspaper made him feel that he was

189

talking to the world. Mrs. Hinds said, " Why isn't that just wonderful " at intervals and watched Pauline. Mrs. Marrowby, who was talking to Pauline, looked at her Donnie, who had wandered away from the table gently whistling a Hungarian rhapsody up the tilted invisible rays of the moon. Pauline listened to Mrs. Marrowby's kind asthmatic anecdotes of the neighbours and caught her breath at the climax of each anecdote. " Oh you dear thing " or " Oh you dear funny lady," said Pauline now and then and covered her face with her hands spasmodically to conceal the fact that she was not laughing. Dr. Marrowby had not been able to come. He had, Mrs. Marrowby said, a confinement.

To Ipsie the light of the moon seemed so intense that she could hear it hiss. A thin sibilance of light seemed to deafen her ears. She had drunk two glasses of champagne. She felt herself to be shut away with Rodd from the others, shut away within clear crystal panes that enclosed exquisite excitement. Every little sound of the meal, the clinking of glasses, the tap of plates, the rustle of Mrs. Marrowby's dress, the whistling of Donnie, reached her, it seemed, intensified by an infinitesimal delay. All sounds were defiant, an insolent and charming snapping of fingers at the moon.

So, she thought, must angels hear the crackling follies of the world, clear, tense, across airless spaces which had devoured their meaning. Angels could shout and sing to God and be gloriously unheard by any one but God. She could say anything conceivable to Rodd. Looking at him she could not believe that she was not intimate with him, that she had not kissed him or heard his secrets.

" I'm not going to marry him," she told Rodd, and her voice seemed to her to run like a little gold wire to his ears. Surely they were alone, one at each end of that wire. Had she said anything at all? It did not matter, he would hear even unsaid things.

" Why I'm glad of that," said Rodd,

looking at her gravely. " I'm awfully, awfully glad of that."

So Ipsie realised that she had spoken with her voice and also that he had replied with his. She even noticed that, being American, he had said " offally, offally glad. . . ."

" You know," said Rodd softly, " I very nearly cabled to you·that you mustn't marry him—the minute I got here."

" I knew long ago I mustn't. I mustn't marry any one."

" *Ipsie*," exclaimed Pauline. " What are you saying? "

" I am saying," said Ipsie, trembling, " that I mustn't marry any one because I have no moral sense."

" Then don't say anything more, for goodness sake," said Pauline. " You are over-excited."

" Yes, so this is the time to say things," said Ipsie. " At this moment I don't care what any of you think, and that never happened to me before. I will not marry Jacob. I will not marry any one. I'm not faithful enough. I'll just have as many lovers as I can."

" Oh nonsense," said Rodd. " You've got the right idea, but don't go too far. . . ."

" Come indoors, Ipsie," said Pauline. " It's my fault," she added to Mrs. Marrowby. " She is weak after her illness, and I should have realised that she couldn't stand the excitement of wine and company."

" I thought at the time that it wasn't wise," said Sophie Hinds. She was of those who, though too cultured to be Prohibitionists, think it at all times rather rash to drink a glass of wine. *The Rubáiyát of Omar Khayyám* was Mrs. Hinds' favourite poem.

Donnie was sitting on a wicker chair at a distance of a few paces from the table. One of his legs was thrown over the arm of the chair.

" Oh what care I for your goosefeather bed . . ."

sang Donnie, staring the moon in the face.

" Come indoors, Ipsie," said Pauline and stamped her foot.

PIPERS AND A DANCER

Ipsie was intensely aware of the beauty
and subtlety of everything she saw.   The
sensitive bowing of the grasses, the glazed
whiteness of the tablecloth, the triple shadows
of the glasses cast by the two lanterns and
the moon, the deeply shadowed sockets in
which Rodd's quick anxious eyes were set,
a cloud like the great feathered wing of a
bird—all these things seemed to come
through a new gate into her sight and by
a new road to her heart.   She was poised
dangerously on the edge of an exquisite
indifference and an exquisite sensibility.
Hate and contempt did not matter now;
she had a wonderful self for a friend and a
wonderful world for a home.

" Yes, I will go indoors," she said.
" Because I don't want to be bothered by
your words.   But I know what I am saying
and I will say it again—I'll never marry
Jacob Heming now."

" Ipsie, be silent.   Ipsie, I command you
to be silent."   Pauline pinched and shook
Ipsie's shoulder.

"I wouldn't command if I were you," said Rodd. "There's been such a lot of commanding done."

"Oh, Lord, Innes," said Mr. Mordaunt. "No need for you to butt in."

"Why not?" asked Donnie unexpectedly. He was apparently practising a dance step in the white air with his swinging toe.

Ipsie went to bed with a merry moonlit hissing in her ears. She had no thoughts, only eyes and ears. She lay on her side looking out into the monstrous and strange night. The tops of the eucalyptus trees were falling very slowly across the luminous sky. Ipsie felt as free of trouble as if she were dead, and as full of essential understanding as if she had never been born.

She saw Rodd walking up the garden path knee-deep in a net made of the shadows of dahlias and heliotrope. She found herself on the verandah.

"Rodd, why did you say, Oh nonsense, about my having lovers?"

"Because every word you said was nonsense," replied Rodd. " Except your refusal to marry Heming. People like you neither want lovers nor could have them if they wanted."

Ipsie said, " I have been too polite up to now to say I wanted lovers. But now— would you think I was showing off if I told you I have no personal sense of right or wrong? I can't say yes or no except in someone else's voice; all my life I've talked in other people's voices—Mother's, my head-mistress's, George Lansbury's, our old house-maid Minnie's, Tolstoi's. . . . I have had no voice, even for natural wants—I don't even know how to ask you—Oh, you lovely Rodd, won't you be my first lover? "

" Certainly not," said Rodd without hesi-tation. " I don't want to be anybody's lover, first or last. I want to be a perfectly respectable husband. I should like you to marry me in a ladylike manner, if you will."

Ipsie stepped back into the shadow. " Look," she said in tears. " I can't even find a lover by moonlight."

Rodd dared not come close to her. " Much simpler to get married by daylight," he said, and hated himself for his voice.

" Much wickeder, much wickeder. . . ."

She looked at Rodd plaintively and critically. No perfection was knocking at her door after all. Rodd's hair was not so thick as Donnie's. Donnie had hair like fur. She had suddenly a pang of delight in Donnie, his thin ankles, the freckles on his face, his slow, high young voice. All men were perfect in fractions—at least they might be so to a woman with no soul.

" Rodd, I've escaped from marriage."

(Oh what care I for your goosefeather bed . . .)

CHAPTER XII

IPSIE felt as if something had been done for her that she would never have dared to do for herself. She felt also that it had been done to some extent bravely, which in itself proved that in doing it she had been possessed —for she knew that she was not brave.

Yet she was ashamed of herself. She shivered every time she remembered words spoken by her under that shimmering moon. She was ashamed of herself because Pauline and Sophie were very angry with her, because Donnie had taken her rebellion for granted, because the Consul had not called again, because Rodd seemed to laugh at her a little. When she saw herself from outside she was ashamed; when she thought of Jacob still peacefully creating Wee Mary somewhere in the flowery mountains she was ashamed; when she thought of herself she gloried.

Pauline was very angry. Pauline felt now that anger was a more powerful weapon in the subduing of Ipsie than love. There was no doubt now. Love was after all a slender rapier, the subtle point of which could be turned aside by armour. Anger was a battle-axe; enemies cannot ignore anger. Ipsie was definitely an enemy now, yet still Pauline counted on possessing her some day, with or without Jacob. So must Goliath have felt when David refused to arm himself in the orthodox way. " I shall have him yet. Weakness is a formidable armour, but it wears thin."

Pauline blockaded Ipsie with silence. When Ipsie entered a room, Pauline, tightening her lips, rose gracefully and left it. Every time this happened Ipsie felt exactly as uncomfortable as Pauline intended her to feel. Ipsie longed acutely for the usual tangle of easy arch talk again. At meals intercourse marched laboriously down two parallel paths—the path between Pauline and Sophie and the path between Ipsie and Rodd. Ipsie's attempts to connect these paths by means of general or direct remarks always proved abortive, though sometimes Pauline was obliged to reply, " I really don't know, Ipsie," through cramped lips. The use of her name unadorned by Pauline horrified Ipsie. Ipsie had lost another member of her insubordinate family of selves —Dear Little Sister Ipsie—and she felt bereaved. She would have been overwhelmed but not surprised to find herself addressed by Pauline as Hippolyta.

Rodd's unfailing cheerfulness did not at all compensate Ipsie for the loss of Pauline's voluminous friendship. On the contrary. Rodd, Ipsie thought, was not even potentially a satisfactory lover. He could not turn the corners of his mouth down even when his hopes were—presumably—blighted. The tight tragic mouth of Pauline seemed much more adequate to a tense situation. Rodd refused to admire in so many words any of the Ipsies her Showman produced for his inspection. He did not leave the Showman, as it were, a leg to stand on, and as a rule showmen are very centipedes in their choice of legs to stand on. Rodd's unspoken answer to Ipsie's unspoken " Will you love this—or this? " would seem to be, " Both a little and neither much."

Yet Rodd, safe in his little entrenchment of pleasant manners, was filled with a kind of contradictory delight in Ipsie. He saw that she was afflicted with emotional instability; he saw that, for some reason unknown to him, she was rarely herself—and least of all herself when she was trying to please. He knew well that he did not know her at all, yet he never doubted that there was someone to know. He was too idle to explore her forest of poses, too idle to appeal to her common sense, too idle to show her that he was not deceived, too idle even to laugh at her much—but he was safe in an absolute certainty that whatever she was, she was important to him. Perhaps he knew that her liking for him was only the reflection of his own feeling on a bright surface—a reflection as sharp and as slight as vanity in a mirror. He noticed at any rate that she only lent him friendship when he praised her. But if he knew what this meant, his gentle optimism hid the knowledge away.

When Ipsie opened her doors she disturbed him much more than when she held herself hidden. He was afraid of introspection, afraid of questions that he could not answer, answers that he could not understand. Sometimes Ipsie would check herself in full pose with a devastating confession. " I was lying when I said that, though I didn't think so at the moment. . . ." " Make me stop talking—I am only copying the heroine of one of Stella Benson's novels. . . ." Rodd would say something like " Be peaceful, Ipsie, now be peaceful. . . . Don't tell tales on yourself." In that mood she made him doubtful and ashamed. She hurt him.

But, though she lived in almost constant

self-criticism, she did not very often criticise herself aloud. Since Pauline now despised her she sought flattery from Rodd. Her vanity was a hungry thing that could never be sated and now was rarely fed. For Rodd, like all young men, was perverse in his homage to his neighbour's vanity. Without intending to show anything but his devotion, he came near to showing Ipsie that she would never find a perfect lover, and why. She became almost aware that her hunger for support was insatiable. A didactic impulse made her wonder whether Jacob might not really be the man designed by God for her simply *because* he would never hear the demanding voice of her vanity—would never even guess her lack. To marry Jacob would have been to marry salutary mortification. She knew that now and rejoiced that she had escaped, as an ascetic might rejoice to find himself at ease. She sought praise of Rodd, despised him when he gave it and herself when he withheld it. Really she sought praise of herself and never found it.

PIPERS AND A DANCER

" Do you suppose the Consul thought I was drunk that night, Rodd? "

" Well my dear, you were."

" Oo Rodd. . . . No, I'm serious. I wasn't even excited. I only had two glasses. Why, I have a stronger head than most men. On the first Armistice night I drank five cocktails running."

" Well, sometimes five cocktails is too much and sometimes it's too little," said Rodd. " In your case on Friday night two glasses of champagne was surely too much. Not a doubt of it."

" Oo, very well. . . . You think me a drunkard."

" I would hardly go as far as that."

" Well," said Ipsie after an offended pause. " All right. I admit I was a little drunk. I certainly saw the tree-tops falling across the sky. But still—that's the way I escaped from marrying Jacob."

" If I were you," said Rodd, " I'd have someone fix up those two glasses of champagne, rampant, as your crest on your teaspoons and the door of your Ford. As it is I'll never despise Mr. Pommery Sec again, and if he runs for President he has my vote."

Rodd, like many persons in love, was just now haunted by charming thoughts of his mother and his childhood. Sometimes he told Ipsie of small things that he remembered —the Adventure of Falling Off the Porch, the Adventure of Being Nearly Caught by the Tide, the Adventure of the Queer Man in the Drug Store Who Must Have Been Crazy. Rodd remembered acutely and rather emotionally. He had not forgotten the intricate perspectives of childhood—but he told of things that had happened, never of things that he had imagined. So Ipsie, whose own childhood was a sort of fungus of eccentric imaginings grown about the dull thin stem of her life, was bored. Ipsie's childhood was very glorious to her although it had not been particularly happy. When she thought of her childhood it was as if she stood in a flame; she stood in a fire of spring beech trees and London palaces,

breaking waves, and the soft tolerant faces of
women and dogs. She was burnt by painful
and beautiful remembrance. Her response
to a story of a pony by Rodd would be a
search in her mind all the time he was
speaking for a glamorous story of her own
about ponies. Behind the expression of
womanly alertness which her Showman
always reminded her to assume, she was
thinking, selecting, discarding. . . . She
was hoping that his story would soon be
finished so that she could tell him a much
better one of her own. His talk of ponies and
falling off porches made her feel ashamed.
Yet, when her moment came, she lacked
words to show him her own past magic.

No efforts or charms on the part of Rodd
could dismiss from Ipsie's mind the uncomfortable silent anger of Pauline. One
day, with a desperate appeal, Ipsie checked
Pauline's dignified flight from a room in
which they found themselves unexpectedly
alone together.

"Pauline, don't go away. Don't treat

me like measles. What have I done to make you so very angry with me? "

" What have you done ! " said Pauline fluently and ardently. " What have you left undone? You've succeeded at last in hurting me to the quick—it's not for want of trying that you didn't succeed long ago. Ever since that morning when I met you— all eagerness and warmth—on the ship in Hongkong, you've been sneering at me, pushing me away. . . . I poured out love and welcome before you from a full heart, and what have you ever given me or mine but coldness, cynicism and neglect? You made light of Jacob's devotion when he worked for you—you forgot him when he was in trouble. You should be thrown out of the society of big-hearted, generous people — you're nothing but a vain and trivial child. . . ."

" I always told you I had no heart," said Ipsie, preening herself a little. To have refused love is very much more picturesque than not to have been offered it.

PIPERS AND A DANCER

" I'm used," said Pauline, " to being loved
by those I love.   I don't love easily. . . ."
Ipsie saw suddenly that Pauline's eyes
had the staring pouched look of eyes about
to cry;   the corners of Pauline's mouth
jerked and were pulled down.   It was indecent, inconceivable, that Pauline should
be allowed to cry.   The imminence of such
a thing crashed through Ipsie's self-satis-
faction as though a mine had been exploded
beneath the foundations of her castle of
vanity.

" Oh Pauline, don't let your eyes look like
that.   I can't bear that you should cry. . . ."
There was no hypocrisy or affectation
about Pauline's distress.   She felt herself
impotent to discover the reason of Ipsie's
refusal to fit into a suitable niche in the
Pauline temple.   She felt defrauded as a
saint might feel who sees at his shrine one
expensive candle unlighted.   Exasperation
was like sand behind her hot eyes, forcing
tears.   And now it was with a rush of
triumph that she saw Ipsie burst into tears.

PIPERS AND A DANCER

Pauline's voice, raised but not broken by distress, was like the viola in place of the usual 'cello. " It seemed," she said, " that Jacob was so defenceless—so far away and in such trouble . . . he ought to have been able to trust us, his womenfolk, to speak for him, to keep his name dignified and fair. That's woman's part—to take care of men. . . . But you're not a woman, Ipsie, you'll never learn woman's rôle. You never will, I think, be anything but a callow little schoolgirl showing off. Women Give, but you only Take. Yet if you choose to toss away the wonderful treasure of Jacob's love —I ought not to grieve. . . . You are not worthy of it. If you are so petty that you cannot realise the wealth of friendship I offered you—why should I be sad? You are the loser. Only . . . to make a public insult of it. . . ."

There was no escaping from the fact that Pauline was significant. Even when she had a grievance she was so large and sure that she had to matter.

PIPERS AND A DANCER

Ipsie cried quite loudly, almost luxuri-
ously. She felt that she had a debt of tears
to pay and she did not stint the tears. She
reproached herself ecstatically; the arguments of Pauline became for the moment
her standard. She admitted the Bighearted
Defender of Men, the Friend, the Giver, as
her ideal for the duration of this mood. She
saw herself as one who could never achieve
such an ideal, never live down her schoolgirl
offences. She would have given away a
thousand Rodds to be again Little Sister
Ipsie, Wee Mary, to be again on the side
of the angels.

Mr. Mordaunt, the Consul, stood at the
French window. Ipsie could not conceal
her tears. She covered her face with her
handkerchief and dedicated a series of
stifled sobs to the reflection that Mr.
Mordaunt would never call her a plucky
little woman again. She had thrown away
all her treasure of flatteries. She had only
Rodd now, and Rodd would not flatter.

" I am sorry to interrupt you," said Mr.

PIPERS AND A DANCER

Mordaunt, looking with dislike and embarrassment at the ambushed Ipsie. " I'm afraid I have bad news for you, Miss Heming. Your brother, it seems, has been taken ill with dysentery on the way home. Colonel Hsu and an escort of soldiers are with him. They are now at a temple about ten hours' ride from here, and Colonel Hsu writes that Mr. Heming cannot be moved until he recovers a little. I'm afraid that was why the bandits made such easy terms. Hsu sends for a doctor with remedies and special food. Marrowby and I are planning to start on horseback in an hour's time. I wondered whether you would care to follow us by chair. We cannot ride fast, as the road is a mountain trail and we have to take soldiers on foot and packhorses. So you would not be far behind and could take advantage of our escort."

CHAPTER XIII

Sophie Hinds at first said, " I must come too. I don't care what the difficulties are." But when she saw the soldiers she said, " Perhaps after all I'll stay here and have everything ready for the dear man." And she cried because she was afraid to go out into the mountains to Meet her Man.

Ipsie watched Pauline and the horsemen go. No one spoke to her. Her thoughts moved quickly about, seeking a refuge. Pauline, as she was lifted up regally in the chair, turned her face away from Ipsie. The chair was carried away above the heads of the Chinese soldiers, who laughed and chattered as they set off in its wake.

Even Sophie Hinds shunned Ipsie. Ipsie could see her sitting in a wicker chair in the garden pretending to sew but really crying. The fact that Sophie had put on a little red hat with raspberries in it to sit and cry in seemed to Ipsie most touching. But Ipsie was suffering from an exaggerated sensibility. As she stood at Jacob's desk she noticed a forlorn sum on the blotting-paper in Jacob's writing. The sum was done wrong. Ipsie cried over that.

Rodd was out superintending repairs to some of the Company's property. The boy sent out to acquaint him with the news had been unable to find him. By the time he came in, an hour after Pauline had gone, Ipsie, in shirt and breeches, was trying clumsily to tie a rolled coat and blanket to the saddle of the Company's pony.

Ipsie looked angrily at Rodd. She gathered her vanity like a torn garment about her and blamed Rodd for its destruction.

" Shall you be long away? " asked Rodd, after watching her for a moment in silence. He felt a fool when he talked to Ipsie in this jocular way, but the truth was, she was the only person in the world who made him feel shy.

" Jacob's dying," cried Ipsie dramatically. " They've gone. They wouldn't let me go too. But I can follow, I can follow and comfort him. . . ."

A series of such dramatic remarks supplemented by Heming's interpreter, who spoke with the nervous polite laugh peculiar to a Chinese passing on bad news, finally made Rodd familiar with the emergency.

" Dear little Ipsie, you can't go off on a long ride like this. You're not strong enough. That was why they wouldn't take you."

" I can catch them up. They've only been gone an hour."

" Ipsie, be kind to me. You imagine so much, imagine me now. Wait at home quietly with me for news. What you want to do is hysterical."

" What I want to do is to pay my debts. Why should I be kind to you? . . . Why should I imagine you? It's Jacob I must remember. Jacob doesn't know I ever forgot him."

Jacob was the only person in her world who did not know of her humiliation and could not despise her. Where Jacob was, there was comfort for her and a rehabilitation.

Rodd said, " Then wait three minutes for me."

While she was waiting Ipsie thought that she was being picturesque now. She could not escape from the sight of herself. She blamed herself bitterly and thought, " If I loved a man I should let him see always the *me* he liked best to see. I couldn't *be* it, I could *seem* it. That will always be the best I can do—just to *seem* the best available."

She could not help feeling gallant and knightly as she cantered along the soft red road behind Rodd. She had a picture of herself that gave her the illusion of a high heart and victory at last. She assured herself that she was impressing Rodd, that she would impress Pauline and Mr. Mordaunt and Dr. Marrowby, that Jacob, even if he died, would die adoring her. Then, even if he died, Ipsie would have a decorative though precarious memory to keep of herself and of him. Even if no one should ever be impressed by her again, she could always be comforted and justified by calling herself one man's beloved. It would be comforting in the same way as cheating at Patience is comforting. She knew well that it would be cheating. Jacob had no beloved though Wee Mary was his "*fiancée*"; Jacob followed no star. Ipsie made an imaginary Jacob; she filled her Jacob with high love and touched his eyes with starlight. So she built up her comfort and her confidence.

The valley was filled with a hot sunlight, and yet the sight of the white ducks swimming in the golden water of the ricefields subtly imposed an effect of spring. Ipsie heard a duck, thinking itself alone, cheeping to itself in the voice of its childhood. There was a touch of youth in the slit smile of a pig as it slept—flaccid and leathery as a half-empty Gladstone bag—in the dust. Even the clear tiny waves blown by the wind across the ricefields had heard, it seemed, a rumour of waves on a pale spring sea on English sands. Over every wall was an unseen beautiful possibility. The valley was full of Chinese commonplaces that England never knew—the roads were beaded with long strings of ox-carts creaking and heaving on elliptical log wheels; the ploughmen were out in the deep ricefields, floating ankle-deep on raft-like ploughs behind the deliberate graceless buffaloes; thin white egrets were written like letters S about the chequered land. Yet, in spite of all these reminders, something unreasonable, something lost and found, something of the excitement of spring at home, was woven in with the bright air. Spring to English people is an English ecstasy. Thoughts of the early spring that England knows—the red expectant colour of hedges in February, the silk corduroy texture of far ploughed fields before the green spring has dyed the air, the cold grey branches that are the vital veins of the forest's body—these

are, for an exile, very dangerous and exquisite thoughts. All springtimes are compounded of all the springtimes we shall
never see again, lost springs that we once
shared with the lambs and the bluebells and
now neither possess nor share. Once we
knew what spring was and, though we shall
never know again, sometimes we can stroke
our lips with primroses and breathe again
our old spring's darling wild lost air.

The road that Ipsie and Rodd followed
left the straight dikes between ricefields and
strayed on low foot-hills covered with Chinese
graves amid coarse faded grass. Some of the
graves were mounds held together by circular
walls. Some were shallow crescents dug out
of slopes, with a stone door in the centre of
each crescent—a door of dwarf size at which
one could imagine little ghosts knocking for
admittance into the secret halls within the
mountains. One could imagine little ghosts
gossiping by moonlight from door to door.
Some of the graves were pinned down by
high weather-streaked pillars surmounted by

little fat stone lions that looked as undignified and as absurdly marooned as Nelson in Trafalgar Square. There were commemorative gateways leading from naked space to naked space. Only a ghost might hope to find home or a welcome behind those gates. On either side of the gates stone lions arched their necks, defying the ghosts who walked through the gates from sunlit space to moonlit space, seeking the known things that ghosts and men can never forget.

Among the graves strode big cranes in groups, looking too large to be real, too zoological to be ghosts.

The road climbed, rose above graves and cranes, divided itself into a network of straggling red trails seeking the line of least resistance. Down in the valley the villages lay, each safely enclosed in its haze of blue smoke and its grove of dark trees. Safety and spring were left behind in the valley. Here on the hill was an old deserted mud fort on a high rocky shoulder. The outer wall was stark and eyeless. In the doorway sat a travelling priest in a blue robe. He wore a black hat like a collar-box, and out of a hole in the top of the hat coiled his sleek snake of hair. The hesitating sound of bells behind the fort betrayed a caravan of mules and ponies resting in the shade, the men sucking at their thick bamboo water-pipes, the ponies straying with a freedom that made Ipsie's pony shriek for a fight.

" Rodd," shouted Ipsie in a happy excited voice that startled him. " What do you do when ponies fight? Put pepper on their heels? " And again a minute later, " Rodd, mustn't it be embarrassing for a mare to have a mule for a child! . . ."

He was as much disconcerted by her cheerfulness as he had been by her tragic mood. He could find nothing but moods in her. Nothing to love but an extravagant and defenceless fallibility. She lacked human ambush; she was a very honest fugitive hiding behind tattered and transparent artifice.

Halfway up a long hill Rodd and Ipsie overtook Pauline swinging slowly in her chair up the plaited strands of the trail. The soldiers behind her and in front of her shouldered their untidy umbrellas with their rifles; they wore dirty towels drooping like hoods under their caps to protect their necks from the sun. One of them was whining a little wordless song. Pauline, enthroned in her swaying chair, lent even her soldiers dignity. When she saw Ipsie her face changed for a moment and she said in a cold voice, " Why have you come? Such a ride for no reason is far too much for you."

" Not for no reason," said Ipsie shortly.

Ipsie was tired directly she saw Pauline. Her sense of humiliation and confusion returned to her. In Pauline's presence she saw herself again as a person who had made a contemptible blunder trying to repair the irreparable. She looked about in order to try and lure her fugitive false courage back again, but she saw sad things only. In the village they passed through, an idiot girl, suckling a baby, smiled through a harelip at the soldiers. The baby's eyes were black

with flies. A dog that was scarcely alive
writhed its cramped body into the sunlight.
Men with sullen and debased faces looked
from doorways, and the only pretty things
the sunlight could find to play with were the
intricately chased silver sheaths and hilts of
the men's daggers.

At the top of the pass all the travellers
must step aside; a dead man claimed the
middle of the road. He lay on his back
with his feet towards those who climbed the
hill from the east; his astonished staring face
was turned sideways; his chin rested on his
shoulder. His turban had been torn off
and the upper part of his body was naked.
The satin skin across his ribs and breast,
his sharp features, the strong muscles of his
neck, and the emphasised irregular formation
of his shaven skull made him seem a miracle
wasted, an intricate achievement thrown
away. He had been a brigand, and the local
guard had laid him there in the hope that
other brigands would see in him a prophecy.

On the other side of the shadowy pass the

whole mountain-side was in sunlight. The sun was slipping down the sky, as it seemed, opposite to and level with their eyes. The madonna lilies and the little faint applegreen flowers of Yunnan edelweiss caught the light and shone in the grass like distant lanterns in dawn-light. The light glazed the broken paving-stones of the road and fretted out from shadow the carving on a row of high stone tablets which stood by the wayside commemorating the names of the builders of the road. At the bottom of the valley a little town lay like gold and brown embroidery draped among trees across a folded gorge.

In this town the travellers were to spend the night.

Ipsie felt her lips swollen with exhaustion as she slid from her pony before the village inn. Dr. Marrowby, standing in the doorway, shouted, "Well, if this isn't our little Miss Wilson appearing like a fairy! You look tired, little lady." His cordial brassy voice gave Ipsie great comfort and she said,

PIPERS AND A DANCER

" Oh no, not really tired," as she stumbled towards him. Her face was stiff with weariness, and she felt that it writhed into an unnatural grimace as she spoke.

" Allow me to assist you into the hotel lounge, madam," persisted Dr. Marrowby, offering her his arm.

In the outer courtyard of the miserable inn Pauline, speaking slow loud English as though she were addressing a gathering of the deaf, gave instructions to confused coolies, soldiers and pack-ponies. Pauline looked at Ipsie for a moment and then threw righteous anger away with a dramatic gesture of her left hand. With her energetic bounding tread that was neither a walk nor a run, she moved to Ipsie's side.

" Dearest childie, you're tired. We'll unpack a camp-bed at once."

It was all over. This was the end of dangerous freedom. Ipsie was again a prisoner in Pauline's favour. She sat on the camp-bed in a room full of dusk. Light pricked in through the fretted wooden

window, enough light to shew the unswept
floor, the rough drawings and writings and
gaping cracks on the wall, the bugs travelling
from crack to crack, the little black pig with
a rope round its waist snuffling in the corner
of the room.   The whole building was askew
and all its walls leaned backward as though
it were a crushed packing-case.   Rodd pulled
in one of the window-frames so that Ipsie
could lean out and discover the inn to be
clinging drunkenly to the brink of a little
cliff which bordered a brawling stream.   On
the opposite bank mud houses were wedged
among low shrubs.   A cord between two
poles supported an array of blue cotton strips,
just dyed, drying in the breeze.   On a ledge
of cropped grass a hoopoe, with a head like
a jeweller's hammer, bowed to its shadow.
When Ipsie called to it it spread the fan of
its crest for a second and then threw itself
frantically into the air and wheeled in a dazzle
of black, white and red stripes like an optical
illusion.

Pauline was like an earthquake in the

place, morally and physically. She walked about the shaking floors sprinkling Keating's Powder and terrifying the innkeeper who followed her everywhere snuffling nervously. The innkeeper was a short, broad man with thin grey wisps of moustache like brackets at either corner of his mouth. His mouth was open and showed very long prominent teeth. He wore a little round scarlet plaster on the middle of his forehead, shewing that he had a headache, probably induced by the arrival of Pauline. He distressed Ipsie by bringing a young live duck to shew her; he pushed it in Ipsie's face with an insistent triumphant gesture saying something that must have meant, " There, never say I don't know my job." The duck, held painfully by the wings, emitted loud bass cries of appeal and fear, yet its face was ill adapted to express trouble and Ipsie's tender heart was almost comforted by the pleased and placid expression of its beak and eye.

" If you will have a smile made of bone," said Ipsie, " nobody will ever pity you at all."

226

But she saved the duck's life, since supper would be due almost before the bird's soul could have fled.

Two candles stuck in bottles illuminated the supper of the travellers, but even by this mean light Pauline never mislaid anything. She was never at fault, never excited; the proud, tragic expression of her face never changed. Nothing was unworthy of her serious and constructive attention.

As soon as she and Ipsie were left alone in their dingy stall she said, " Now, my Ipsie is going to sleep on the camp-bed. Old Pauline's tough bones will rest well enough on this board-and-trestle-ex-supper-table."

Ipsie was too weary to enter into a competition of nobility with Pauline.

Pauline drew the trestles and boards close to the camp-bed and the two women, after wrapping themselves in coats and blankets, lay down side by side. In the darkness they could hear the rats running across the court-yard; they could hear the echoing brave noise of the stream like fairy cavalry clattering down the gorge.

"Dearest," said Pauline gently, stroking Ipsie's fingers under the blanket. "It has been a cloud, a blindness, that separated us. Love has triumphed."

Ipsie wondered if love must always be a ridiculous word in her ears. "Jacob . . ." she stammered, but she could find nothing to say of Jacob since she could not say that she wanted to be loved by him but not married. The word Jacob seemed like the word *love*, ridiculous. It always seemed unkind to talk of Jacob—even kindly— behind his back.

Pauline, curiously, had not thought of Jacob. She had dismissed from her mind the possibility of a marriage between Jacob and Ipsie. She had been feeding her pride with congratulations on Ipsie's surrender to herself—Pauline. However, a noble-sentiment rose naturally to her lips.

"Yes, dear faithful Jacob . . . we will both defend him now. In spite of what people say, darling, I think real spiritual faithfulness to one woman is a man's virtue rather than a woman's. Good men love their own woman and think all the rest fools; woman loves all men and thinks her own man a fool."

Neither could find anything definite to say about Jacob. Oblivion seemed to enclose Jacob and to detach his name from words. Ipsie could only think of the black hairs that grew in his ears. She wondered drearily what colour his pyjamas were. While Pauline stroked her fingers Ipsie hated all men—their hairiness, their coarseness of skin, their flannel pyjamas. . . .

A grey cloudy light awoke the travellers at six and before the sun could unravel the tangle in the sky they were on the road.

Rodd avoided Ipsie. His attitude of mind from the beginning of the journey had been, " Oh very well then, very well. . . ." He was too self-confident to feel humiliated by Ipsie's ominous reconciliation with the Hemings. " Very well then, very well. . . .

PIPERS AND A DANCER

If you really prefer inferior persons—go
ahead. Not so very valuable after all. . . ."
And she was not valuable to him. His
heart was wrung by her, but she was not
splendid, not a miracle, not a lost dream to
him. He wanted to have her for his own;
he did not at all want to be possessed by her.
He despised her a little and would have
defended her from his own contempt. She
could not break his heart.

At midday a terraced village suddenly
shewed itself on a steep yellow meadow
cupped like a crater in a hill-top. At the
foot of the village there was a small dark
lake, and at the edge of the water a row of
soldiers, naked except for their caps, were
washing their clothes. The ascent had been
very steep and the four riders had been
obliged to climb slowly on foot. So that
Pauline in her chair was close behind and
Dr. Marrowby could shout to her, " This is
the place."

Pauline stopped her chair and ran before
it up the hill, her generous cloak blowing

back from her shoulders. "We must find him quickly."

Outside the archway, which led through the mud wall of the village, a basket hung and in it were a couple of withered human heads. These, which were the heads of brigands, were a sort of signature denoting local approval of the ideal of law and order.

A soldier stood in the gateway. He said something that none of them could understand and led them down an alley between blind yellow walls. The steps of a temple were shaded by a great pale cotton tree. Little brown pottery elephants, horses and lions were balanced upon the roof ridges; a short repeated note, half bell, half drum, was whispered from the altar.

A soldier at the door of the temple smiled at Dr. Marrowby and said one word again and again, leaning forward and looking in the Englishman's face as if to watch for the first light of understanding. The soldier's smile seemed familiar to Rodd; the interpreter had worn that smile as he spoke of

Jacob's illness. Rodd could see, too, an abrupt slackening in Dr. Marrowby's stiff carriage. So Rodd knew what the word was.

Dr. Marrowby laid his hand on Pauline's arm as she passed him.

"Miss Heming . . . we are too late. . . ."

Ipsie followed Pauline into the shrine on the other side of the courtyard. An old woman, who had been beating the drum before the gaudy gods, looked curiously at the newcomers and went away. There was a green tree in the courtyard and through its moving leaves the sun tossed and shifted fragments of light, like coins of silver running through a miser's fingers, across the body of Jacob.

Dignity was not difficult to Jacob now. It was a thin, still Jacob, unnaturally long; his large feet hung over the end of the boards on which he lay. His face, which looked faintly surprised, seemed about to awake; his lips, it seemed, might part and say, " Well, I have slept well. We can go home now." Only his feet, drooping on limp ankles over the edge of the boards, would most certainly never move again.

For a moment Pauline looked at him quite coldly, seeing in him, as it were, a theoretical brother only. " Jacob," she said in a quiet commanding voice, and though she knew he was dead she waited for his eyes to open. " He ought to have done what I wanted," she thought. With a pang that was not the pang of bereavement she visualised him living in the reflected light of her recommendation, married to Sophie Hinds, safe, discontented and prosperous in Peking. " He should have done what I wanted. I was right. He would have been alive now if he had listened to me." She felt a dreadful triumph in her justification. So Death, walking bleakly on the pale scarred mountains of China, had proved her right. Jacob had died in the glaring presence of the blue and yellow plaster gods saying, " Pauline was right, Pauline was right . . ." to the rhythm of the temple drum. Well, this was what happened to people who

would go their own way. Even as a child
he——

Pauline's mask of calmness suddenly
twisted and dissolved. The barrier across
which she had strangely seen the body of
her brother was gone. As a child—as a
child he had been after all a darling slave to
her. Not death but thirty years of life had
stolen him away—that child who used to sit
on the red carpet in the middle of the ring
round which his clockwork engine ran.
*Pauline, Pauline, look what you've done—
you've trodden on the junction. Well, you silly
Javie, it's time you put those babyish things
away now. Time for lessons.*

Now he had put them away. He had put
all his toys and lessons away.

" Javie . . . Javie . . . Javie. . . ."

CHAPTER XIV

IPSIE left Pauline alone at the foot of the altar beside Jacob's body.

Jacob looming prostrate in a faint haze of blue joss-smoke was at once intimate and strange to Ipsie, at once greater and smaller than he had ever seemed before. She sat among the piled knotted roots of the great tree in the courtyard and, hiding her eyes with her hands, remembered Jacob's deep dead face. The face of Jacob was before her eyes so intimately that she felt that she had been married to him in all but body. He was a man whose socks she should have darned and at the same time a lover on whom the fine honour of death had been conferred. He might for the first time be loved by a romantic. Dead, he had found a way into her imagination; alive, he had not sought it. Had Conrad then informed that dead face in the tawdry temple dimness? Was perfection then always just behind the thin releasing hand of death, removed always by nothing more than a stride, nothing more than a beat of the heart?

She looked up and saw Rodd standing in the shade of the tree, wrinkling his forehead, slapping the tree-roots with his riding-whip. Poor Rodd had a magnificent rival now. Rodd, it seemed, was dead and Jacob victoriously alive. Rodd's face was in Ipsie's sight like a dead leaf, his pale brown gentle face, his light eyes that could never have held her safely.

As Rodd sat down beside her she watched his face and erected a memorial of confused thought to his memory. Watching people's faces—that was her life, watching for Ipsie in people's faces. Rodd's face was a mask of friendliness; she had never found herself there. He had fatally left her to create herself. It was Jacob who had very nearly found her, very nearly made her real. And now Jacob would be buried in the mountains with his dreamless and desirable Wee Mary beside him. Nobody would ever make a dream of Wee Mary again. Only Ipsie would survive and Ipsie was anybody's thing. " I'm lost, I'm lost for ever now. I'm anybody's thing. I'm at the mercy of twopenny gods."

Rodd sat beside her although, for the first time in his life, he was conscious of not being wanted. " Ipsie, he was a fine fellow in many ways but don't forget, he's the same fellow now as when he was alive."

" Oh no, he's not."

" Keep me a little in your thoughts, Ipsie," said Rodd. He would be like steel in her soft thoughts.

Pauline came out of the shrine and stood on the steps looking about with wide-open bewildered eyes, but she did not at once seem to see Rodd and Ipsie.

Rodd's mind was twisted and disordered by violent anger against these Hemings, these insatiable Hemings, living or dead. There had been only one wild and elusive thing in the world for him, only one thing that he did not understand, only one fairy— and this the Hemings would seize and cage.

As Pauline saw them and came towards them Rodd swore that he would not let go; he would not leave Ipsie alone with the formidable Pauline. For even he could see that Pauline was especially formidable at this moment. She had never before looked childlike or accessible. Ipsie took Pauline's hand awkwardly and they both looked at Rodd.

" Look, then, look . . ." thought Rodd. " I shall hold on for all your lookings."

Pauline pressed Ipsie's shoulder strongly with her arm. " Dear little girlie . . . my Javie's choice. . . ."

Ipsie felt herself promoted as she stroked Pauline's hand. Here was a newly created Ipsie for the Showman—One who brings Comfort to the Weak and Sorrowful. Pauline was consenting to be weak and sorrowful.

Now that Ipsie had seen Pauline surrendering there seemed to be nothing lacking about this wonderful woman. The essential inferiority of Pauline was at last hidden from Ipsie by Pauline's weakness. She felt Pauline's sorrow like a wound in her own heart. She remembered with great pain the habitual arch and arbitrary expression of Pauline's eyes. Everything in the world seemed worthless until that look should return to Pauline's eyes.

" Pauline . . . adorable, adorable Pauline."

Pauline turned to Ipsie with a look of intense triumph in her eyes. " We won't leave each other again now, my dearest," she said. " I had a plan as I knelt beside our dear Jacob trying to reach his mind. You and I are real sisters now. Listen, we will go away by ourselves to Arizona and breathe the pure air into our lungs that are tired of China and get well and some day find our hearts healed again. Oh, the healing sunlight that is striped by the cactus shadows. . . . We will live on a ranch and milk cows

and ride horses and wade in flowers. . . .
Little sister, what do you say? "

She leaned forward and looked closely
into Ipsie's face.

" She smiles . . . she smiles . . . she's
my little girlie now. . . ."

When Rodd saw Ipsie's face he told
himself finally, " I can't hold her."   He did
not care then.   Nobody in the world mattered
really to him.   Nothing in the world except
his ôwn death could touch the core of his
being.   The hard, happy bones of him were
safe, though surrounded by a network of the
nerves of love and pity.   " I don't care, I
don't care," he thought obstinately though
he was trembling with anger.   Let Ipsie
throw herself to the lions then. . . .

Stupid, mumbling words came to his lips.
" But she was to have lovers. . . ."   Yes,
but now she would be walled up alive in
benevolence.

Lovers. . . . Ipsie thought of Jacob
perfected by death.   She thought of Conrad
walking strongly towards a storm against a

PIPERS AND A DANCER

wind between creaking and shouting trees.
Lovers . . . how far were these lovers
from a mystery in a double bed. People
like Rodd fitted into striped pyjamas. But
lovers. . . . Her voice was very low. "No.
I'll be idle now."

And something in her face showed Rodd
the truth at last.

"Why, she's not alive. There was nothing to hold on to. She's lost life and God
knows what she's found instead. Reality's
the only thing she can't imagine. She's a
fairy. She's a fairy. Nobody can hold her.
Nobody can hold a fairy."

Suddenly alone, he was amazed to find
himself weeping for the loss of his fairy.

THE END

Printed in Great Britain by R. & R. CLARK, LIMITED, Edinburgh.